The
HOUSE
of
HUNGER

Dambudzo Marechera

WAVELAND

PRESS, INC.

Long Grove, Illinois

For information about this book, contact:
Waveland Press, Inc.
4180 IL Route 83, Suite 101
Long Grove, IL 60047-9580
(847) 634-0081
info@waveland.com
www.waveland.com

Photo Acknowledgments
Pp. i, ii, and 9 by Flora Veit-Wild

Acknowledgments
Every effort has been made to contact copyright holders of material reproduced in this book. Any omissions will be rectified in subsequent printings if notice is given to the publishers.

10 digit ISBN 1-4786-0473-5
13 digit ISBN 978-1-4786-0473-0

Printed in the United States of America

7   6   5   4   3   2   1

DAMBUDZO MARECHERA and *THE HOUSE OF HUNGER*

Charles William Dambudzo Marechera was born in June 1952 in Vengere, the township of Rusape, in the east of the then Rhodesia. He was the third of nine children in a family which became destitute once his father was killed in a road accident in 1966. He gained entry to one of the first secondary schools to be opened to blacks – the Anglican St Augustine's Mission School at Penhalonga. In 1972–73 he was inscribed as an English major at the University of Rhodesia. From 1974 he studied further on a scholarship at New College, Oxford, from which he was sent down in March 1976 to live out his exile in Britain in a succession of squats for another six years. He contributed to several publications, including *The New African* and the London *Sunday Times*, hammering out the first draft of *The House of Hunger* on his portable typewriter in a matter of three weeks.

First Street reading during the Harare Book Fair, 1983

Notoriously on his return to independent Zimbabwe in February 1982 with a Channel Four crew intent on filming him, he was confronted with the news that his second novel, *Black Sunlight* (1980), had been banned. When Lewis Nkosi viewed the film at the 1983 Zimbabwe International Book Fair, he called it 'a marvellous, scandalous document, recording the scars left by colonial society on one of the most original talents yet

i

to emerge in African Literature.' Marechera became noted as a tramp, writing in public on park benches, as recounted in the journal of his return to his native land included in *Mindblast*, published in 1984. He lived to see his *The House of Hunger* taken as the mouthpiece of his generation and then of the new internal exiles post-independence. Later he could afford a bedsitter in the centre of Harare, where in January 1987 he was diagnosed with pneumonia as a complication of AIDS. In May that year, in an interview with Kirsten Holst Petersen, he noted: 'I lead a very solitary life, and so most of the time I am simply reading, in here or outside.' He died in August that year, aged thirty-five.

Reading at the College of Music in Harare, 1984

The House of Hunger first appeared in the Heinemann African Writers Series in December 1978, with an edition soon published by Pantheon in New York. A translation of the whole sequence into German followed after his appearance at the Horizonte Festival in West Berlin in 1979, with others into Dutch and French, with 'Protista' going into Norwegian and 'Burning in the Rain' into Portuguese. For the original edition he was awarded the Guardian Fiction Prize in 1979, jointly with Neil Jordan (£250 each). Reviewing it for *The Guardian*, one of the competition judges, Angela Carter, remarked: 'It is indeed rare to find a writer for whom imaginative fiction is such a passionate and intimate process of engagement with the world.' The first edition included the title novella, with nine additional sketches and short stories, a few of which were intended to be read as interrelated with the main text. Here some of the makeweights have been omitted in favour of later pieces written to complete

The House of Hunger cluster. They are 'The Sound of Snapping Wires' (first published in *West Africa* on 7 March 1983), with the three last essays, all unpublished at the time of his death. The prefatory 'An Interview with Himself' of 1983 is also an addition here.

Kole Omotoso in *West Africa* (14 September 1987):
> 'Dambudzo Marechera's life provided the material for his art. His existence, to those intent on their business of living, seemed dedicated to dying. On 18 August he finally completed the process that began with his birth.'

David Caute in *The Southern African Review of Books* (Winter 1987–88):
> 'The writer Dambudzo Marechera died in Harare at the age of thirty-five. A brilliant light, flashing fitfully in recent years, is extinguished. He once wrote: "It's the ruin not the original which moves men; our Zimbabwe ruins must have looked really shit and hideous when they were brand-new."'

Dieter Riemenschneider in *Research in African Literatures* (Fall 1989):
> 'Marechera's first-person narrator in a story like "The Slow Sound of His Feet" is unable to restore a life that is both meaningful and worth living. He paints a harrowing picture of the individual suffering of a person who bears much resemblance to the author himself.'

Dan Wylie in *English in Africa* (October 1991):
> 'Marechera is the misfit. His *The House of Hunger* is

a characteristically turbid, angst-ridden, dadaesque story virtually unparalleled in African fiction, by a profoundly dislocated writer living in a shattered, repulsive environment of mindless violence, raw sex, filth and madness.'

Lisa Combrinck in *Work in Progress* (August 1993):
'Above all, Marechera believed that the task of the writer in a changing society was to be honest, true to him- or herself and never hypocritical. Young South – and other – Africans who read Marechera will probably, like their Zimbabwean counterparts, embrace his works as a militant young lion who bravely criticised the government in the post-uhuru period.'

Jean-Philippe Wade in *Alternation* (1995):
'*The House of Hunger* is one of the most important texts to emerge from Southern Africa in recent decades. It should be on every school and university syllabus, because these powerful stories challenge just about every complacently hegemonic view of what "African Literature" is.'

Wole Soyinka, nominating *Scrapiron Blues* as his book of the year (1996):
'A profound, even if exaggeratedly self-aware writer, an instinctive nomad and bohemian in temperament, Marechera was a writer in constant quest for his real self.'

A K Thembeka in *Laduma* (2004):
'He was a black who read all *their* books, and let

them know it in the relentless stream of quotes that littered his prose. The literati rewarded him, not for his achievements, but for his "struggle".'

Kgafela oa Magogodi in *Outspoken* (2004):
    'my song grows from the ground
    where Marechera rose to write'

Stephen Gray (2009):
    'The central text in this revised *The House of Hunger* collection is well enough established by now as the unforgettable, virtuoso accomplishment of African writing in English of the 1970s. Indeed, with its overlapping scenes of horror and of humour, it rattled the staid and timorous establishment like a refreshing outburst from a mighty imagination, setting itself impressively free. Supported here as it is now by various satellite pieces to complete the cluster, it reads all the more finely.'

CONTENTS

AN INTERVIEW WITH HIMSELF

Which writers influenced you?
I find the question oblique, not to the point. It assumes a writer has to be influenced by other writers, *has* to be influenced by what he reads. This may be so. In my own case I have been influenced to a point of desperation by the dogged though brutalised humanity of those among whom I grew up. Their actual lives, the way they flinched yet did not flinch from the blows dealt out to us day by day in the ghettos which were then called 'locations'.

Who are these 'They'?
They ranged from the few owners of grocery stores right through primary school teachers, priests, deranged leaders of fringe/ esoteric religions, housewives, nannies, road-diggers, factory workers, shop assistants, caddies, builders, pickpockets, psychos, pimps, demoralised widows, professional con-men, whores, hungry but earnest schoolboys, hungry but soon to be pregnant schoolgirls and, of course, informers, the BSAP, the police reservists, the TMB ghetto police, the District Commissioner and his asserted pompous assistants and clerks, the haughty and rather banal Asian shopkeepers, the white schoolgirls in their exclusive schools, the white schoolboys who'd beat us too when we foraged among the dustbins of the white suburbs, the drowned bodies that occasionally turned up at Lesapi Dam, the madman who was thought harmless until a mutilated body was discovered in the grass east of the ghetto, the mothers of nine or more children and the dignified despair of the few missionaries who once or twice turned up to see under what conditions I was actually living. This is the 'they'. The seething cesspit in which I grew, in which all these I am talking about went about making something of their lives. These are the ones who influenced me – through their pain, betrayals, hurts, joys.

3

You mean you observed but did not participate?
How can you 'observe' a stone that's about to strike you? That was my relationship with the then Rusape 'society'. I was the drunken brawls. I was my father one night coming home with a knife sticking out of his back. I was the family next door being callously evicted because the father had died – it was to happen to my own family too. I was my father when some sixteen year old twit, white twit, insulted him. I was all those who were being evicted from the surrounding white farms and being dumped and dumped anywhere. I was the fellow student dropping out because the school fees just could not be found. I was in the horrible dark nights (the street lights never worked), I was the ghostly lamentations and wails when someone died and you knew they would have to bury him in that rubbish dump they used to call the Native Cemetery. I was the young primary school teacher strutting everywhere with an important air. I was all my age group when we formed ourselves into gangs and gang warfare broke out into real fights with sticks, bricks, stones, knives. I was a cowboy, an Indian, a GI, a Second World War British commando officer – those dark days of succulent escape from our cheap and humiliating surroundings. But what terrified me most – it was the seed of Marie's blindness in *Black Sunlight* – was the sight of blind parents being led around by their five year old little girl – they had nowhere to stay – sometimes they slept in the stadium, sometimes at the Railway Station – but the police were always after 'vagrants'. It was so pitiful and pity was not easy to come by in the ghetto of those days. Then there were the disabled – no one cared – I didn't care. To my eyes all this was our normal condition. The condition which later drove most of our fellows into Mozambique to become freedom fighters and I to become a writer.

4

Why a 'Writer'? Not many Blacks were?

Hmm. The dull and brutish ghetto life was always there. Fights, weddings, arrests, church services, the school-bell summoning us to assembly, summary evictions, football, insults, athletics, grim poverty, netball, the line of convicts going to and from hard labour on some white bastard's lawn or farm, playing golf behind the notorious women's hostel – the hard physical facts of day to day ghetto life. There was this too much, this cruel externality – you could not escape it. But there was the rubbish dump where they dumped the garbage from the white sections of the town – a very small small-minded, very racist town. I scratched around in the rubbish with other kids, looking for comics, magazines, books, broken toys, anything that could help us kids pass the time in the ghetto. But for me it was the reading material that was important. You could say my very first books were the books which the rabidly racist Rusape whites were reading at the time. Ha-ha, my most prized possession was a tattered Arthur Mee's *Children's Encyclopaedia* – very British Empire orientated but nonetheless a treasure of curious facts about the universe and the earth. There were jingoistic British Second World War comics. Superman. Batman. Spiderman. Super this, super that. Mickey Spillane, James Hadley Chase, Peter Cheyney, Tarzan things and Tarzan thongs. I had these two friends, Washington and Wattington, twins. They had built 'offices' of mud and tin and cardboard, offices about two and a half feet high. They had a children's typewriter. They were the Chairman and General Manager. I was the office boy. We had a library there – of books and comics salvaged from the dump. Every day it was the rubbish dump – and then the offices. Washington typed down meticulous records of each day's acquisitions. See what I mean? There was the typewriter, there were these books. After school every day that was what we did.

That's when you thought of writing?
Not exactly. But the connection was made. You see? I was very young – I am talking of the period when I was still in primary school, when I was six years to ten years old. At this time I did not think blacks could become writers. I did not see a book by a black author until I was in Form One, at boarding school – Ngugi's *Weep Not Child*. And that was mind-blowing – that sealed and signed the earlier fumbling connection. I suddenly knew what I would do with my life – write stories, poems, plays. Write!

You started writing when you were eleven?
I would have done, but something happened. My father was killed. Our family was evicted from the ghetto house. It may have been a ghetto house but it had been our centre. And there was no father any more. Mother was a nanny. There we were – nine kids for her to look after. She was sacked. I was in Form One. Where would the fees come from? What did it mean that father was dead? What did it mean to not have a home? It was the beginning of my physical and mental insecurity – I began to stammer horribly. It was terrible. Even speech, language, was deserting me. I stammered hideously for three years. Agony. You know in class the teacher asks something, my hand shoots up, I stand, everyone is looking, I just stammer away, stuttering, nobody understands, the answer is locked inside me. Finally the teacher in pity asks me to please sit down. I was learning to distrust language, a distrust necessary for a writer, especially one writing in a foreign language.

Did you ever think of writing in Shona?
It never occurred to me. Shona was part of the ghetto daemon I was trying to escape. Shona had been placed within the context of a degraded, mind-wrenching experience from which apparently the only escape was into the English language and education. The English language was automatically connected with the plush and

seeming splendour of the white side of town. As far as expressing the creative turmoil within my head was concerned, I took to the English language as a duck takes to water. I was therefore a keen accomplice and student in my own mental colonisation. At the same time of course there was the unease, the shock of being suddenly struck by stuttering, of being deserted by the very medium I was to use in all my art. This perhaps is in the undergrowth of my experimental use of English, standing it on its head, brutalising it into a more malleable shape for my own purposes. For a black writer the language is very racist; you have to have harrowing fights and hair-raising panga duels with the language before you can make it do all that you want it to do. It is so for the feminists. English is very male. Hence feminist writers also adopt the same tactics. This may mean discarding grammar, throwing syntax out, subverting images from within, beating the drum and cymbals of rhythm, developing torture chambers of irony and sarcasm, gas ovens of limitless black resonance. For me this is the impossible, the exciting, the voluptuous blackening image that commits me totally to writing.

Struggle with language – that's your purpose?
Yes and no. Language is indissolubly connected with what it is that constitutes humanity in human beings and also, of course, with inhumanity. Everything about language, the obscene, the sublime, the gibberish, the pontificatory, the purely narrative, the verbally threatening, the adjectivally nauseating – they are all part of the chiselling art at the heart of my art, the still sad music ...

What was the cultural milieu in the ghetto?
This was the sixties. Upheavals in politics, the surge of black nationalism, the banning of ZAPU, the early attempts at armed struggle. I was too young to know. Even when Nkomo arrived to

hold a meeting and my sister took me with her; and there were all these police and reservists firing teargas shells and I was choking, dying, not knowing what was happening, why I was running, everybody running, the police dogs coming, running, my sister screaming for me to get up and *run*!

The Beatles. The Rolling Stones. Cliff Richard, Elvis Presley. The Shadows. Every transistor radio seemed turned up full blast. There was this small 'township' hall where we had bands playing smanje-manje, jazz, rock 'n' roll – one of them was called *The Rocking Kids*, all ghetto youths who had taught themselves to play guitars and drums and the saxophone. And every Friday there was a film show. Hoppalong Cassidy. Gene Autry. Tarzan. James Bond, Ronald Reagan. Fuzzy. Woody Woodpecker. And Wow – Charlie Chaplin. There were the weddings, the rousing singing of heart-crushing breakteeth Shona songs and games about love and courting. Kids playing 'House', playing at being engaged. Improvising games that revolved around the duties of marriage, the conflicts of growing up. There we were, learning cigarettes, beer, sex and of course the use and abuse of violence.

You could say the beer hall was the cultural centre. Itinerant guitarist/singers would play in there. People like Safirio Madzikatire, who is now one of our top national singers and is also a more than competent actor for both radio and television. People like Kilimanjaro. The kids who were to become guerrillas. Kids who were to become mujibas in the struggle. Kids who were to sacrifice their All for freedom – all growing up here.

(1983)

1984 POSTSCRIPT

I am afraid of one-party states, especially where you have more slogans than content in terms of policy and its implementation. I have never lived under a one-party state, except pre-independent

Zimbabwe, Ian Smith's Rhodesia, which was virtually a one-party state. And what I read about one-party states makes me, frankly, terrified.

I think writers are usually recruited into a revolutionary movement before that revolution gains whatever it's seeking. Once it has achieved that, writers are simply discarded, either as a nuisance or as totally irrelevant.

I don't know that the writer can offer the emerging nation anything. But I think there must always be a healthy tension between a writer and his nation. Writing can always turn into cheap propaganda. As long as he is serious, the writer must be free to criticise or write about anything in society which he feels is going against the grain of the nation's aspirations. When Smith was ruling us here, we had to oppose him all the time as writers – so, even more, should we now that we have a majority government. We should be even more vigilant about our own mistakes.

As soon as one talks about a writer's role in society, before you know where you are, you are already into censorship. Most writers in Africa, I suppose in most Third World countries, are usually seen to be in conflict with governments. So much so that governments in Africa tend to automatically suspect a writer of not being loyal. The idea that a writer should always be positive, that's always being crammed down one's throat. A writer is part of society; a writer notices what is going on around him, sees the poverty every day. How can you whitewash poverty?

Marechera in 1985

9

THE HOUSE OF HUNGER

I got my things and left. The sun was coming up. I couldn't think where to go. I wandered towards the beer hall but stopped at the bottle-store where I bought a beer. There were people scattered along the store's wide veranda, drinking. I sat beneath the tall msasa tree whose branches scrape the corrugated iron roofs. I was trying not to think about where I was going. I didn't feel bitter. I was glad things had happened the way they had; I couldn't have stayed on in that House of Hunger where every morsel of sanity was snatched from you the way some kinds of bird snatch food from the very mouths of babes. And the eyes of that House of Hunger lingered upon you as though some indefinable beast was about to pounce upon you. Of course there was the matter of the girl. But what else could I have done, when Peter flogged her like that day and night? Besides, my intervention had not been as disinterested as I would have liked.

Yes, the sun came up so fast it hit you between the eyes before you knew it had risen above the mountains.

I took off my coat and folded it between my thighs. The way everything had happened no one could in future blame their soul-hunger on anybody else. Mine was already hot and dusty in the morning sun and I didn't know what, if anything, I could do to appease it. But my head was clear; and when the black policemen paraded and saluted beneath the flag and the black clerk of the township sauntered casually towards the Lager trucks and a group of schoolchildren in khaki and green ran like hell towards the grey school as the bell rung I felt I was reviewing all the details of the foul turd which my life had been and was even at that moment. The policemen were dismissed. Their sergeant was a cocky six-footer, lean and hungry and sly like a chameleon stalking a fly. The House of Hunger had not as yet had much to worry about this particular chameleon. There had been unpleasantnesses

11

though. The old man who died in that nasty train accident, he once got into trouble for begging and loitering. And then Peter got jailed for accepting a bribe from a police spy. When he came out of jail Peter could not settle down. He kept talking about the bloody whites; that phrase 'bloody whites' seemed to be roasting his mind and he got into fights which terrified everyone so much that no one in their right mind dared cross him. And Peter walked about raging and spoiling for a fight which just was not there. And because he hungered for the *fight* everyone saw it in his eyes and liked him for it. That made it worse for him until his woman got pregnant and the schools inspector said she couldn't teach in that state, and Peter threatened to crunch the sky into nothing and refused to marry her because he wanted to be 'free'. It was during that disgrace that father took something mildly poisonous and sickened visibly before our eyes and didn't speak a single word, though we knew he knew we knew it was all to pressure Peter into the marriage. She was after all sweet and childish and big with his sperm and we all couldn't believe Peter's luck. It was at this time my sixth form like other sixths rushed out into the streets to protest about the discriminatory wage-structure and I got arrested like everybody else for a few hours: which meant fingerprints and photographs and a few slaps on the cheek 'to have more sense', though the principal restrained his bile and only gave us a long sermon on how necessary it was to get qualified before one deigned to put up the barricades. At this time I was extremely thirsty for self-knowledge and curiously enough believed I could find that in 'political consciousness'. All the black youth was thirsty. There was not an oasis of thought which we did not lick dry; apart from those which had been banned, whose drinking led to arrests and suchlike flea-scratchings. I had got over aching for the un-attainable Julia who had been left in my charge by my best friend. I was at that point where it's no use fussing and fretting whether one could with a will find some money and dare the unknown terrors of VD – with a little help from dagga. I braved it one stormy night and survived to regret it. Peter of course understood.

'You aren't a man until you've gone through *it*,' he said.

And I agreed and smiled ingratiatingly because he knew where the cure was – at least, how to get injections in decent secrecy. The experience left me marked by an irreverent disgust for women which has never left me. Never again would I suffer wholeheartedly for any woman.

But not everyone was scratching everyone else's back. There were arrests en masse at the university and when workers came out on strike there were more arrests. Arrests became so much a part of one's food that no one even turned a hair when two guerrillas were executed one morning and their bodies later displayed to a group of schoolchildren.

There was however an excitement of the spirit which made us all wander about in search of that unattainable elixir which our restlessness presaged. But the search was doomed from the start because the elixir seemed to be right under our noses and yet not really there. The freedom we craved for – as one craves for dagga or beer or cigarettes or the after-life – this was so alive in our breath and in our fingers that one became intoxicated by it even before one had actually found it. It was like the way a man licks his lips in his dream of a feast; the way a woman dances in her dream of a carnival; the way the old man ran like a gazelle in his yearning for the funeral games of his youth. Yet the feast, the carnival and the games were not there at all. This was the paradox whose discovery left us uneasy, sly and at best with the ache of knowing that one would never feel that way again. There were no conscious farewells to adolescence for the emptiness was deep-seated in the gut. We knew that before us lay another vast emptiness whose appetite for things living was at best wolfish. Life stretched out like a series of hunger-scoured hovels stretching endlessly towards the horizon. One's mind became the grimy rooms, the dusty cobwebs in which the minute skeletons of one's childhood were forever in the spidery grip that stretched out to include not only the very stones upon which one walked but also the stars which glittered vaguely upon the stench of our lives. Gut-rot, that was what one steadily became. And whatever insects of thought buzzed about inside the tin can of one's head as one squatted astride the pit-latrine of it, the sun still climbed as swiftly as ever and darkness fell upon the land as quickly as in the years that had gone.

The lives of small men are like spiders' webs; they are studded with minute skeletons of greatness. And the House of Hunger clung firmly to its own; after all, the skeletons in its web still had sparks of life in their minute bones. The girl, of course – and how I felt for her – clung rebelliously to her own unique spirit. The severity of the beatings could not stamp the madness out of her. And though he finally beat her until she was just a red stain I could still glimpse the pulses of her raw courage in her wide animal-like eyes. They were eyes that stung you to tears. But Peter with his great hand swinging yet again to smash – those eyes stung him to greater fury. It was all a show for me; I knew that, and that made it worse for her because she had told me she would never give *that* up.

And Peter firmly but calmly said: 'I'll beat it out of you yet.'

At this her eyes flared up in that sad but obstinate way she has.

'Go on, then!' she cried, ducking her head on to her breast so that the blow missing her eye knocked her sideways. I heard something – a cat – scream in agony.

At that moment I could have sworn that *she* was putting on a show for me. I laughed. That was my first mistake. There had been other mistakes which had led up to all this, but this was the first major one. Peter glared at me, fist raised. I heard it again – a cat – in utter agony.

'And what are you sniggering about, bookshit?'

It was not a question. And as I looked at him I could have sworn that he too was laying it on thick just for me, though in a brotherly way. It almost made me laugh again. But I drew the candle closer to the book I was reading and after a moment found the passage I had reached.

But he blew out the candle, plunging the room into darkness. I could feel his stale breath clinging closely to my face. I could hear through the window children saying 'Break its neck'.

'I asked you a question, Shakespeare,' he said out of the darkness.

I said nothing; I was amazed at the swiftness of his attack. His hands grabbed my shirt-front.

I did nothing.

He spat full into my face and shoved me backwards so that I fell with the chair, hitting my head against the wall. I heard him clattering out of the room. I lay still until I could no longer hear his footsteps. He seemed to be walking down the street, probably towards the beer hall. It was then that I realised that the baby in the next room was hollering its head off and must have been screaming for quite some time. But neither the girl nor I moved. She was panting painfully somewhere in the dark of the room. I could only think how very young she sounded. She had a strange name.

I called out to her: 'Immaculate, are you all right?'

But there was only silence.

'Why did you come back?' I asked. 'You know it's always like this.'

After another long silence she said something like ssshh.

'What? I can't hear you.'

'Don't talk,' she said.

15

In the next room the baby continued to scream. A heavy stone rattled upon the roof: our neighbour's children were at it again. Another stone – it must have been a brick – thudded on to the roof. A shadow streaked by the open window hurling something – a furry and wet thing that struck me in the face. I had thrown it clear from me before I realised what it was. As I dashed to get it a stone cracked where I had been lying and broke against the chair. I thrashed through my coat for matches, found them, and lit one. The light of it, flaring angrily, at once lit up her face which was swollen and streaked with blood from cuts on her lips and cheekbones. The flame burnt my fingers and I thrust the spent match out of the window and lit another. This time she was holding out a stub of a candle. When it was lit I saw she was leaning over the furry wet thing which had struck me. It was my cat. It was dead. The fur was not only spattered with blood but also half-burnt, as though our neighbour's children had even tried to burn it before flinging it through the window.

She had got up and put the candle on the table and was looking abstractedly at the overturned chair.

'Did he hurt you?' she asked.

I shook my head.

'And you?' I asked rather pointlessly.

'I'll be all right in a moment,' she said. 'The baby – he didn't touch the baby?'

'No.'

'I wanted to see you,' she said.

I couldn't think what to say. I felt vaguely scandalised. She always talked like that – as though I was someone she had dreamed up. I didn't want to scrub up the passion and the beatings of her cruel life. And yet it was I who had started it all. My disinterested intervention – that's how I had put it to myself. How was I to know she would take it into her head to take me at my word? I felt so bitter that I laughed at the cruel sarcasm that rules our lives.

The hollowness of my laughter seemed to startle her. I said hastily: 'I was just thinking what a fool he will look when he finds out.'

'A fool ... who?'

'Why, my brother, Peter,' I replied rather foolishly.

She frowned.

And I thought happily: she has seen through me and will have nothing to do with such corruption. But I was as usual deceiving myself, for her face cleared and her tiny biscuit frown turned into a dimple as she tried to smile. The fool!

'You're such a child,' she said, caressing my arm.

I pushed her away, muttering something about my dead cat which in my suppressed fury I kicked towards the door and then gave it a final hefty kick which sent it flying way out into the yard. I wished with all my soul it was her I had kicked out into the night. The grey matter of my brains was on fire with loathing for her.

The little tricks and turns of the weather not only seemed to be personally directed against me but their venom was of such an unpredictable character that I – how long ago it is now! – made a point of ignoring their unwanted attentions. Friends who acted out of character affected me in the same way. I could not of course cut a tropical storm dead, but the ignominy of scuttling for shelter from what one felt was after all peculiarly part of oneself was an indignity I could not forgive. And I was by this creating for myself a labyrinthine personal world which would merely enmesh me within its crude mythology. That I could not bear a star, a stone, a flame, a river, or a cupful of air was purely because they all seemed to have a significance irrevocably not my own. Therefore I ignored them but recreated them with words, cadences, lights, murmurings and storms of air escaping the blast that came from 'up there'. I was all mixed up. I found the idea of

17

humanity, the concept of a mankind, more attractive than actual beings. On a baser level I could not forgive man, myself, for being utterly and crudely *there*. I felt in need of forgiveness. And those unfortunate enough to come into contact with me always afterwards consoled themselves and myself by reducing it all to a 'chip on the shoulder'.

'You'll soon get over it,' they said. Like the way babies get everything before they become immune to that strange malady, growing up.

In the House of Hunger diseases were the strange irruptions of a disturbed universe. Measles or mumps were the symptoms of a malign order. Even a common cold could become a casus belli between neighbours. And add to that the stench of our decaying family life with its perpetual headaches of gut-rot and soul-sickness and rats gnawing the cheese and me worrying it the next morning like a child gently scratching a pleasurable sore on its index finger.

How could I just get over it, for heaven's sake?

What began as a little stream of moral experiment had swelled into the huge Victoria Falls of a cancerous growth.

But I disdained to call it that. It was a sort of life, I suppose. It was *me*, not anyone else.

'You mean the world owes you a living?' Peter asked slyly.

I did not answer because the answer was there for anyone to see: the chill of a vicious winter night blasting through the old gate of that House of Hunger – the answer was chillingly creeping through the marrow of my bones and trickling surely into the grey matter of my brains.

My mother used to tell her friends that I had been a 'frantic' baby and that whenever anyone so much as touched me I would become apoplectic with fear. Or hysteria. But perhaps she was exaggerating, because she always mentioned this whenever she was showing off my school reports.

18

'You expect nothing but evil from anyone,' Peter said, yawning. It was the day after the VD injections had started to work on me and I had stopped to think of my penis as a diseased appendage.

'Any good you get from people you'll have to pay for later,' I said. I stretched out my legs and lit one of those cigarettes that seem to be made from a hotchpotch of tea leaves rather than heart-of-the-veld tobacco. I was not at all thinking of what I was saying or why I was saying it.

'What do you think *she* expects in life?' I asked absently with a sort of transparent cunning, which of course Peter easily deciphered.

He even feigned ignorance.

'Who?' he asked nonchalantly.

'Immaculate.'

'What she gets,' he said and laughed like a crow that has fed well.

I felt cut to the quick by his gluttonous merriment. And I almost asked him cruelly who he thought was really the father of his baby.

At this point mother rushed in. She looked like sour milk. Peter muttered something under his breath about it being 'one of her days'. She crossed over my outstretched legs and sat down at the table. Her face was long and haggard, scarred by the many sacrifices she had taken on our behalf.

She began to talk in her usual bass voice: 'The old man's dead,' she said.

It sounded both cryptic and ridiculous. I laughed long and loud.

But she regarded me without the slightest interest. 'He was hit by the train at the rail-crossing,' she said. 'There was nothing left but stains.'

That hoarse bass voice of hers had not always been like that.

She blamed it on the way she had 'come down in the world'; which was merely a euphemism about her excessive drinking. Drinking always made her smash up her words at one particular rail-crossing which – as had really happened with the old man – effectively crunched all meaning or significance which might be lying in ambush. She liked nothing better than to nag me about how she had not educated me to merely sit on my arse. And when nagging me her language would take on such an earthy hue it made me wonder why I ever bothered to even think about humanity. The expletives of her train of invective smashed my body in the same way as the twentieth-century train crunched the old man into a stain.

'I sent you to University,' she said. 'There must be big jobs waiting for you out there.'

'Tell that to Ian Smith,' Peter butted in maliciously. 'All you did was starve yourself to send this shit to school while Smith made sure that the kind of education he got was exactly what has made him like this.'

I did not like this so I began to whistle 'Little Jack Horner Sat in a Corner'.

Peter, as is usual when something indistinct disgusts him, farted long and loudly and spat in my general direction, and muttered something about capitalists and imperialists.

'And the bloody whites,' I added, for this trinity was for him the thing that held the House of Hunger in a stinking grip.

The foul breath of our history, he said.

I threw my coat over my shoulders – not unlike the way night suddenly covers the late afternoon sky – and got up to buy another beer. It was crowded in the bottle-store but the barman, recognising me – he had done so already, it's just that he is the type of person who takes his time even when greeting his own mother-in-law – shouted: 'Terrorist! Gandanga – it's a beer, isn't it?'

My face-muscles creased into a delighted mask as I stretched out my hand over the mass of shoulders to give him the money.

He laughed painfully: 'No, no. It's on me,' he said.

I took the beer, spilling a little on to wide crimson shoulders which suddenly turned angrily.

'Sorry,' I mumbled quickly and then stopped: 'Why, it's – !'

The coal-black face above the crimson jacket split into a toothy smile. It was Harry. At school he had always tortured me about my lack of 'style' – and lack of money. In the sixth form he had the cubicle next to mine and was forever recounting harrowing stories about 'where he was at with the chicks'. He knew all the city slang, all the slick scenes, and at the throw of a dice could name every name worth knowing in 'showbiz'. But when we found out that he had been working for the Special Branch in its infiltration of student organisations we one stormy night gagged him, bound him like a crumb of stale toast and, after a rather dramatic journey out of the dormitory area, beat him up so thoroughly that he took to his bed and for at least three hours did not open his mouth to boast about where he was at.

And now here he was already gripping my arm with a tongue-scalding coffee joy. I had last seen him reeling through the Student Union Xmas Ball. He slapped his thighs and laughed a whiff of crude innocence. He is one of those people who go through life with the firm belief that no one, but nobody, can help liking them in whatever circumstances. And he was right to a certain extent. Immaculate was his sister.

We came out of the bottle-store arm in arm, the way Jesus and Judas must have been when they both knew each other's secret. The sun struck gently against the swirling dust. A cloud of flies from the nearby public toilet was humming Handel's 'Hallelujah Chorus'. It was an almost perfect photograph of the human condition.

Solomon the township photographer is now a rich man. His studio at the back of the grocer's is papered from floor to ceiling with photographs of Africans in European wigs, Africans in miniskirts, Africans who pierce the focusing lens with a gaze of paranoia. The background of each photo is the same: waves breaking upon a virgin beach and a lone eagle swivelling like glass fracturing light towards the potent spaces of the universe. A cruel yearning that can only be realised in crude photography. The squalor of reality was obliterated in an explosion of flashbulbs and afterwards one could say 'That's me, man – me! In the city.'

Harry must have made a lot of photographers rich. Before I developed a sense of discrimination about clothes I had always admired his loud brash colours, his toothpaste set of character, and his massive confidence in high-heeled shoes.

'You and me,' he said drinking, 'we're civilised.'

It was for him the pinnacle of a life well lived, that word 'civilised'. I had sat down on the ground and he was. looking down at me with a quizzical smile.

'Sit down,' I said.

He laughed.

'There're no chairs around, man,' he said, and stuffed a fist into his trouser pocket. He said: 'I've got to see some chick later so I mustn't mess up my clothes.'

'What chick?'

'Guess,' he winked.

I decided to brave it: 'A white chick?'

He laughed: 'What else, man?'

His arm swept the panorama of barbed wire, whitewashed houses, drunks, prostitutes, the angelic choirs of God-created flies, and the dust that erupted into little clouds of divine grace wherever the golden sunlight deigned to strike. His god-like gesture stopped abruptly – pointing straight at the stinking public lavatory.

'What else is there, man?' he repeated.

I think I saw his point.

Immaculate had once asked me the same question – but with a very different emotion from that of her white-chicked brother. She and I had gone down the valley and crossed the river and walked up the ancient stone tracks that led up to the old fortifications which our warlike ancestors had used in time of war. The soft skin stretched effortlessly over the pain behind her delicate oval face. We were looking down over the valley, down upon the township in which we lived.

'What else is there?' she repeated.

And her hands were hurting me. No photograph can ever record the fire of that moment. But I – the fool! – clutched at the tiny straw of loathing for her. It was not possible that a being like her could have been conceived in the grim squalor of our history. She made me want to dream, made me believe in visions, in hope. But the rock and grit of the earth denied this.

'I can't afford it,' I said.

She looked up quickly.

'If it's money – ' she began, frowning.

'Money!' I laughed bitterly like a misunderstood child.

And yet money was certainly part of it. There was no possibility of loving, eating, writing, sleeping, hating, dreaming even – no possibility without money.

But those heroes, those black heroes of our time ...

She was looking at me anxiously, her fingers digging into the small of my back. Something in her gaze seemed to stab into me like a pitchfork, to stab and to pierce into my guts until she suddenly drew back and it seemed dragged out my entrails.

I would have fallen off that ledge had she not caught me. We both fell heavily on to the rock of certainty; we lay still.

But Harry was saying: 'My white chick is full of sugar. She is a full-bodied wine with a touch of divinity, that's what she is, my chick.'

'But has she got a vagina?' I asked, puzzled.

He looked at me oddly.

I hastily changed the subject: 'How did you meet her?'

'That Xmas Ball, man,' Harry winked. 'That's where! Man, has she got it!'

'Got what?' I demanded and yawned unconvincingly.

'Everything,' he said. 'She's got everything nigger girls don't have.'

I closed my eyes. I could see the red curtains of my soul.

'Nigger girls are just meat,' Harry said. 'And I don't like my meat raw.'

And then he looked at me pointedly as he said: 'Of course it's another thing when a man is starving for pussy.'

I bit my lip irritably and muttered something obscene.

'That's it, man. Swear it out of your system. It does a man good to swear.' he said.

'Cheers!' I said, and drained my glass.

In an instant Harry had disappeared into the bottle-store. I leaned back against the msasa tree and lay still, trying not to think about the House of Hunger where the acids of gut-rot had eaten into the base metal of my brains. The House has now become my mind; and I do not like the way the roof is rattling.

I remember coming home one day. Running with glee. I forget what it was I was happy about. And though it was a rather dismal day – the sky looked as if god was wringing out his dirty underwear – I was on heat with living. I burst into the room and all at once exploded into my story, telling it restlessly and with expansive gestures, telling it to mother who was staring. A stinging slap that made my ear sing stopped me. I stared up at mother in confusion. She hit me again.

'How dare you speak in English to me,' she said crossly. 'You know I don't understand it, and if you think because you're educated ...'

She hit me again.

'I'm not speaking in Eng – ' I began, but stopped as I suddenly realised that I was talking to her in English.

I rushed out of the room and sat down heavily on a rock in the garden. I was trying not to cry. I jumped up and rushed back into the room and, dragging my box from under the bed, took out my English exercise-books and began to tear them up with a great childish violence. Mother watched me in silence. When I had finished she took out my food and set it before me. I pushed it away.

'I'm not hungry any more.'

'Are you sure?' she asked.

'I'm not hungry,' I insisted, trying not to look at the food.

'Well, I am,' she said.

And she began eating it right there, with loud smacks. I watched her in silence. She made me feel so hungry I could have strung myself up from the roofbeams. When she finished she actually licked the plate with her red tongue and licked each of her fingers in turn and gave a little belch of delight. It made my soul tear suddenly like the old cloth in the Temple. And the room seemed to move – but it was me getting on to my feet. I stood up before the room turned round completely. As I did so, something chinked in my pockets. I still had some money! I threw the bits of torn exercise-books back into my box and walked out to the grocer's, where I bought three brand new exercise-books and a half-loaf of bread with a bit of butter. On my way home I passed by Harry's and he was good enough to lend me his English books so that I could copy out of them all the things I had torn up.

When I got back father was eating at the table, munching slowly and thoughtfully like an old elephant. Mother was telling him about the torn exercise-books. He did not look at me. I sat on the floor as far away from them as was possible, and began to eat the bread while flicking through Harry's books. A chair, drawn back, creaked. I tensed. I stared stonily at the floor, at the books. The blow knocked my front teeth out. The blow knocked the bread clear across the room. He was rubbing his knuckles thoughtfully and looking down at me as though I was a cockroach in a delicatessen. I flung myself at him but his long aim reached out and grabbed my forehead so that my flailing hands and my kicking rage did not even brush against him. He held me like that until I was so tired I could not move. And then he pushed and I fell back into my corner on to the exercise- books. Staining them with blood.

I was nine years old then.

Harry's blood-red coat loomed before me. He gave me a beer. And he drew a red handkerchief from his pocket and blew his nose. He looked at his snot.

'She gave me that, you know,' Harry said.

'Who?'

'Who else but my white chick.'

I stretched my lips into a painful smile.

'Your lips are cracked,' Harry said frowning. 'There's blisters on them.'

I ran my tongue over them; but he shook his head: 'No,' he said, giving me a chapstick. 'Use this.'

I used it.

'You can keep it,' he said, drinking and spilling pink drops on to his red tie.

He looked at his digital watch.

I was staring at the orange-red roof of the stinking public toilet.

'The bar's opening now,' he said. 'Let's go in and drink the good lord's health.

I dusted myself the way a browbeaten mongrel performs its hasty toilet. We aimed straight for the wide and gleaming gates that lead to the muses.

Harry said: 'Let's go into the lounge. The Special. *The*

Cocktail Party. T S Eliot.'

Harry drew himself up like Achilles sizing up Troy.

'If it's Styx I may as well go down in style,' I mumbled thickly.

'What?'

'I said you've got style, Harry.'

'Style,' he repeated appreciatively. 'Ah, style.'

He rapped on the counter with a silver coin.

'All my life I've been in the kraal slaughtering cattle like Ajax,' I said.

'Who?'

'In Homer,' I said. *'The Iliad.'*

'Ah, ancient Greece,' Harry concluded for the benefit of the barman, who was staring fixedly into my incredible face.

When the drinks were ready we lingered at the counter.

'You literary chaps are our only hope,' Harry began.

I choked politely on my drink. Then we are sunk, I thought.

I began to feel like those stale mornings when the cold wind writhes about purposelessly as if there was nothing but air in the gleaming casket of creation. The sick juices were welling up in me, making me want to vomit. And that blasted barman was still staring with great interest into my face.

'You look well,' Harry said. 'I've never seen you look so well.'

'It's been a long time,' I mumbled.

I creased my face with the effort of fighting the sickness that was welling up and eating my insides with the corrosive acids of gut-rot. The stitches had not tightened yet.

'Yes, long time no see,' Harry agreed.

He clinked glasses with me.

'Drink up,' he ordered politely.

I did. The glasses were promptly filled up again.

The barman blurted out in my face: 'Aren't you the ...?'

But Harry, frowning heavily, cut in: 'No, he isn't. Let's find somewhere to sit.'

We did, our backs to the wall and facing the door – Harry insisted on that.

But as we sat down, something metallic clinked in the region of Harry's waist and slid into view: handcuffs. Without looking down or anything Harry shifted his body and scuffled them out of sight.

I took out a cigarette and lit it slowly. The smoke made my eyes smart.

'You shouldn't smoke those, you know,' Harry said, and brought out an expensive brand. 'Put that thing out and try one of these.'

'Later,' I said absently.

'Have the packet, anyway. I've got another. Now, tell me,' Harry said, 'how is she?'

I feigned ignorance. 'Who?'

'My sister.'

'Well.'

'Not from what I heard.'

'Gossip.'

'She told me herself.'

'What about?'

'You and her and your disinterested intervention.'

The tinfoil of my soul crinkled.

'My dear fellow, what can she possibly tell you about me? She's my brother's woman,' I said, and tossed off my drink with an excessive show of worldly confidence.

He regarded me with an aluminium amazement and decided to change the conversation.

'Your reputation seems to have outstripped the facts,' he said thoughtfully. 'Did you see the adoration in that greasy barman's eyes? Look, he's still staring. There. Your poetry has mesmerised him.'

I looked up. As I did so the old cloth of my former self seemed to stretch and tear once more. The pain flashed through my head and like a cold hand squeezed my bloody lungs. (What shall I see when the cloth rips completely, laying everything bare? It is as if a crack should appear in the shell of the sky. The human face in close-up is quite incredible – Swift was right. And what of the house inside it? And the thing inside the house? And the thing inside the thing inside the thing inside the thing? I was drunk, I suppose, orbiting around myself shamelessly. I found a seed, a little seed, the smallest in the world. And its name was Hate. I buried it in my mind and watered it with tears. No seed ever had a better gardener. As it swelled and cracked into green life I felt my nation tremble, tremble in the throes of birth – and burst out bloom and branch.)

When I finished washing the blood of the cat from my hands she once more began to caress my arm. Her face had puffed out and one eye had closed up. And the holy bitch still dreamed, still hoped, still saw visions – why! I had never seen anything like it.

'Can't you see we'll all come to a sticky end if things go on like this?' I asked desperately. I could hear the baby still crying in the next room.

'I just wanted to see you again,' she said quietly. And then as an afterthought she added: 'Do you know you are – arrogant? Very.'

What has that got to do with it? I thought. But that was not the time to show my sharp little teeth. Besides, death's handful of iron filings was coldly burning my brains out; some magnetic force in the air was resolutely turning and turning them through my very thoughts.

Fragment of this huge emptiness
Whose pulses sparkle in man's eyes
What excavation discovered you so rudely into the light?

'What ?' she asked. She looked extremely puzzled.

'A poem,' I said.

But Harry leaned forward and upset my glass.

'What poem?' Harry was waiting expectantly.

'A poem I'm writing,' I said, 'I've just recited the first three lines.'

And again that oblique look: 'You did nothing of the sort. You've just been sitting there like something in a trance. What three lines, anyway?'

I could not for the life of me remember them.

Harry clucked sympathetically. He jabbed a finger into my face.

'Now, poetry,' Harry began, 'is the soul of all civilised nations. Verse. Tiger tiger burning bright. In the forest of the night. The falcon cannot hear the falconer. Things fall apart. When the stars threw down their spears what rough beast ...'

He paused for breath; and then continued: 'I've never forgotten that poem,' he said thoughtfully.

His hot breath hissed into my face as he leaned forward confidentially. 'I've never told anyone this,' he said in a low voice, 'but I write *lyrics*.'

(The emphasis he put into the word 'lyrics' startled the barman who, astonished, dropped a glass which shattered behind the counter.)

I stared at Harry. I did not know whether to laugh or cry. But he deciphered my gaping look as admiration.

'Thanks, old boy,' he said in a low voice. 'It's not every town that honours its own lyricist. *Drinks!*'

And the barman danced a swift minuet.

Harry's glass clinked my glass and we drank each other's health.

I suppose I was beyond worrying about health; dead souls have no such worries. An extreme case of the left hand not caring a piss about what the right hand was doing. I was, I knew, a dead tree, dry of branch and decayed in the roots. A tree however that was still upright in the sullen spleen of wind. And caught among the gnarled branches were a page from Shakespeare's *Othello* and page one of the *Rhodesia Herald* with a picture of me glaring angrily at the camera lens.

But Harry was saying something.

'... in the evening edition,' he said. 'I couldn't believe it, but you've always been rather a closed fist.'

'No. It's just that I've no friends.'

Harry stared; wounded.

'I've always liked you, you know,' he said.

'Don't let's get personal,' I said, feeling sick. 'It might be painful.'

He cleared his throat.

'Let's get drunk instead.' He swallowed phlegm.

I laughed and said: 'That's more lethal.'

I looked up. The barman's eyes bored into mine. The laughter was hurting my gums; something was twitching uncontrollably above the barman's left eye. I got up hastily and, escaping into the toilet, just made it to the bowl where I was violently sick. As I came out, wiping my mouth with the back of my hand, I collided with two massive breasts that were straining angrily against a thin T-shirt upon which was written the legend ZIMBABWE.

'You better watch where you're going, dearie,' she said.

'Sorry,' I mumbled, darting past her.

But she clutched my arm.

'Or better still, buy me a drink – a brandy for Zimbabwe,' she said.

This time I scrutinised her face and – 'It can't be Julia!' I exclaimed.

'In the flesh like the Word,' she said, twinkling her eyes as though posing before an expensive camera.

My cheeks slowly sank down into my boots.

'Come and join us,' I said in a small still voice.

Julia was the girl who had been left in my charge when I was in the sixth. Now she had straightened out her hair with that damnable hot comb. Her lips were a flaming crimson, like blood. There were darkened patches around her eyes, and false lashes. The eyebrow pencil seemed to have completed the transformation of my old Julia into a beer hall doll. And she immediately clashed with Flash Harry by exclaiming: 'Isn't he the police spy whom you chaps beat up behind the dormitory?'

Harry was not at all amused.

'You're just a nigger whore,' Harry flashed. 'What do you know?'

She appealed to me.

'Yes,' I said yawning, 'it's him all right.'

'Look sonny,' Harry said, getting up.

'Why don't you run along to your goddam white chick?' I suggested.

But Harry has got style. He drew himself to his full height and was about to position his arms akimbo when – his handcuffs once more rattled into view.

There was a dead silence for exactly seven seconds.

I used the pause to savour old Julia's make-up; her massive breasts that were stamped by the gigantic legend of Zimbabwe. With weapons like that Africa could – my thoughts were shelled like groundnuts by Julia suddenly breaking out in the most scornful laughter I've ever heard. Harry cracked, and took a coal-like step towards her; but before he could actually hit her I was between them, drawing slowly upon my stub of a cigarette.

'I'll try one of your cigarettes now, Harry,' I said.

I opened the packet he had given me and lit one. It was as good as he had said. All of a sudden I was a child again, enjoying myself. Mentally dancing with glee. And Julia ...

'A brandy is it, Julia?' I coughed smoke into Harry's face.

His Wankie face.

His eyes were glowing like live coals. He managed a little spittle of a laugh from the side of his mouth. 'Yes,' Harry said, 'I'm just going to see my white chick. But I'll be back – for you,' he added pointedly.

It flashed through my nerves: 'Harry, if you come back there'll be no more fencing,' I said.

'Are you threatening me? There are witnesses ...'

'Barman,' I said, 'a brandy for the lady. And a beer for myself.'

The barman winked.

When I turned round with the drinks Harry had gone. She took the drinks and put them on the table and, eyes twinkling as of old, she threw her arms around my shoulders and brought her face close enough not to touch.

'Hi,' she smiled.

'I thought you were never coming,' I said. 'I waited and waited the whole of yesterday.'

'I had to fight to get anything out of father,' she said. 'He was in one of his moods. You know how difficult he is when he is like that.'

'Your passport ?' I whispered.

'Sssshh.' She kissed me lightly on the cheek and we sat down. She dipped her little finger into my drink and licked it quickly.

'Well, what was Harry on about?'

I hesitated.

'They must have some leads I suppose, and they've sent

him to ...'

'But we know,' she said slowly.

'That picture in the newspapers,' I reminded her without conviction.

'They probably know I'm the weakest link in the chain,' I added.

'We had to feed that to them,' she said.

I looked up sharply.

'Did you have to tell them about my being ...'

'It was my idea,' she said.

And her eyes were sparkling. I was staring at the legend on her breast and thinking about black heroes.

'And did you have to paint yourself up like that?' I demanded weakly.

Her eyes opened wider; there were stars in them. I had to change the conversation.

'Any trouble getting through?'

She bit her lip ruefully: 'A little,' she said.

She was looking closely into my face.

'I left the House of Hunger today,' I explained vaguely.

'What about the girl?' she insisted.

'Immaculate? With a name like that she'll survive.'

'Do you still – are you still ...?'

'I never was. You know I can't, at least not forever. Now and then, perhaps.'

'At least that's honest,' she said. Her voice was brutally sarcastic. She said: 'You disgust me.'

My cheeks slowly rose from my boots and settled back in my face.

'Now, Julia, what have I done wrong?'

'You didn't phone like you promised. And I kicked up a fuss so fierce that father said if ever he saw you again in his house he would – congratulate you.'

'He's daft.'

'Why didn't you phone?'

'Trouble at the House,' I sighed theatrically. 'You know what that is.'

'Your disinterested intervention?'

'Yes. It backfired.'

She bit off a corner of her forefinger nail. Her eyes quickened.

She asked again: 'What about the girl?'

'She's got lots of courage. But only the kind that's the quickest way into the madhouse.'

'You *are* arrogant,' she said.

I lit her cigarette. I was watching a tiny spark of combustion pulsing in her eyes. I still held the flaming match, between my thumb and second finger.

'You've never forgiven me that filthy film,' she said.

She dabbed at her face, messing up some of the eye-shadow.

I did not bother to answer; after all I had also made one with a girl called Patricia.

'Then why do we always ...?'

'Yes,' I repeated pointedly, 'why do we always quarrel?'

I still held the burning match.

Unaccountably Julia burst out laughing. Her laugh is very infectious – the barman crackled hilariously like crisp bacon frying spatteringly.

And when she raised her glass and the highlights of it flung their spears into my watery eyes my life gleamed for an instant, like a searing flash of pain.

It was Philip who had left Julia in my charge; and when we joined him at the university things had soured a little. The gist of it was Philip made a scene and declared that I was a beer-guzzling little Judas; Julia stormed out of the room to return a few seconds later wielding a broom and scared Philip to death. Whereupon I fled the campus and wandered about in the streets until I found a black night-club that was still open. There I drank heavily but something was wrong and I couldn't get drunk. It was the place: all garish colours and lights and a band of half-naked girls dressed up in leopard skins and gyrating out some coarse smanje-manje. The big man at the microphone was not so much singing as farting out in an unnatural bass voice. The walls were all plastered with advertisements for skin-lightening creams, Afro wigs, Vaseline, Benson and Hedges. There was one in particular of a skin-lightened Afro-girl who was nuzzling up to her coal-black boyfriend and recommending the Castle Lager. As the music boomed against the advertisements and the arse colours and lights flickered on and off I lost count of time and simply soaked myself with the stuff. I was no nearer to discovering the authentic black heroes who haunted my dreams in a far-off golden age of Black Arcadia. And then it was time to leave. I lurched out through the doors into the cold night-horrors. A taxi came to a halt. I stumbled into the back seat, mumbling where I was going. But someone, a very fat skin-lightened woman – one of the dancers – jumped into the car and sank against me smiling.

'You want to forget?' she whispered a gust of gin into my incredible face.

Before I could say anything she tapped the driver on the shoulder and the taxi shot off into the night. After many turns and side-turns – it seemed to me we were going round in circles – I no longer knew where on earth we were. But the taxi, slowing down, stopped before a bright blue door which was lit up by a naked light bulb. She got out first and then walked round to open my door. She paid the driver who then drove up the ill-lit street and swerved sharply out of sight. She took out a key and in a second we were taking off our coats in a narrow hallway and she was whispering something indistinct: '... you must be a good boy now.'

My head hurt with the sudden glare of white light. The floor was painted charcoal black but the walls were spotless white. In the far corner an effigy of Ian Smith dangled by the neck from a large butcher's spike. She caught me smiling.

'You want to forget?' she asked.

I could not place her dialect but I understood her. I was sure now.

'No,' I said firmly.

'Good.'

The lights went out.

That night all the lights I had known flashed through my mind. The pain was the sound of slivers of glass being methodically crushed in a steel vice by a fiend whose face was very like that of my old carpentry master who is now in a madhouse. The skin-lightened dancer – she was burning, burning the madness out of me. The room had taken over my mind. My hunger had become the room. There was a thick darkness where I was going. It was a prison. It was the womb. It was blood clinging closely like a swamp in the grass-matted lowlands of my life. It was a Whites Only sign on a lavatory. It was my teeth on edge – the bitter acid of it! It was the effigy swinging gently to and fro in the night of my mind. And the pain of it flared into flame, flickering like a match; for a moment it lit up the room, making the shadows of the naked dancer and me leap quickly across the ceiling and fuse into an embrace. Leaping like ecstasy grown sad – a violence slowly translating into gentleness.

But the match died out and history was the blackened twig of it. The fine grains of that burnt-out insurrection were the stories of those black heroes among whom my story was merely one more skin-lightening pain.

Is the pain of the mind greater than that of the body? The

friends whose hurt looks have flung me back into living like this – little cubes of ice burning through my mind ...

'You're burning your finger!' Julia exclaimed.

I threw the almost burnt-out matchstick into the ashtray.

Julia had darted up to order more beer. The bitch. But I could never swear by convincement like the Quakers, though certainly a divine spark seemed to be her primum mobile. My expletives are raked out of me by a liking for blasphemy.

'I swear because of a lack of adjectives to use,' I said as she handed me a drink.

'Fuck!' she exploded casually and sat down.

For some reason I began to recount to myself trivial incidents which had left me feeling like a cat thrown without extreme unction into a deep well.

One day I had been invited to give an informal – illegal – speech to a group of vagrants. As I warmed up to my theme – I knew all the boys there, except one who throughout sat apart looking very gloomy and frowning darkly at my rhetorical effort – something clicked in my mind and I began to harangue them, trying to rouse their minds by giving them examples of heroism on the part of our nationalist guerrillas. As usual I overdid it. I realised this when I became aware of the venomous silence that had come upon my audience. The flood of political rhetoric escaped like a cloud of steam out of my crater of a mouth, leaving me dry and without words. At that point the boy who had been sitting apart stood up and advanced menacingly towards me. There was on his face no natural landmark but one twisted mark of violent intention. The boys behind him were as compact and expectant as celebrants at a particularly bloodthirsty rite. And behind them the late afternoon sky nickered and dipped, abandoning me to my unhappy fate. The rapid twilight seemed to propel the angry youth towards me. He struck me with his fists twice upon the same side of the jawbone. My spectacles, glancing off, tinkled in the grass. He struck me again, twice, on the same spot. I remember I was terrified, not so much by the pain but by the likelihood that if the Trojan traitor went on hitting me like that I would probably fall and pass out. I turned the other cheek. This time the boy was less sure of himself as he struck me again. I stared straight into his eyes and muttered something about 'calling it a day'. But that rekindled his fury – he was hitting me the way a hailstorm destroys a garden of flowers. I could feel various pains and aches all over my body. The boys, moving closer, closed in a tight circle around us. The boy had become as wild as a man who is trying to stamp out a tiny bug which he can scarcely see. At this point a low growl wheezed among my vagrant audience. The boy paused uneasily and realised as I did that the mood of the boys had swung to my side. Like me, he had overdone it. In a moment the vagrants flung me aside and jumped on his back. The boy was instantly lost to sight in a mass of fist-flying, boot-kicking, head-butting; even his squeal of fear was rudely choked by the grunts of my saviours. The boy is now a permanent invalid; as if that was not enough, his mind from that day refused to budge in any direction and he is now also what they call an idiot. But he seems to remember the cause of his misery, because the other day he nearly beheaded my mother as she was returning from a wedding feast.

'Life is a series of minor explosions whose echo dying out settles comfortably at the back of our minds,' Peter said as he reviewed my sixth form report.

I agreed reluctantly.

Peter was holding the offending report by the scruff of the neck and through it shaking me back and forth the more to emphasise my vagrancy.

Immaculate was thoughtlessly staring at the sock she was darning. I bowed my head in a vain attempt to strangle the laughter that was roaring at the back of my throat and cackling out through my ears.

Peter was looking at me the way an ugly boy inspects a sudden rash of pimples.

Finally he threw the offending report at my feet.

'Get out of my sight!' he shouted, like Jesus saying 'get thee behind me, Satan'.

I was about to precipitate myself out of the room when he called me back.

There was a grim silence.

But the guillotine did not fall.

I dared to look upwards at the blade.

He threw a handful of dollars at me: 'It's the best report I've ever set my eyes on,' he said. 'Go and get drunk.'

I smiled, crumpling up the tinfoil of my delight.

I returned, hours later, stone sober, with a parcel under my arm. He was screwing her underneath the table. Before I could retreat Peter said crossly: 'Come in: sit down. This is home, man. Anyone would think you'd wandered into Daniel's lions' den.'

I sat down still clutching my parcel. He looked pointedly at it.

'What's that.'

'Some books by Robert Graves,' I said.

He stared the way one does on discovering some shameful family secret; or the way one does when one finds out that one's best friend is actually a murderous lunatic who has escaped from a grim and satanic institution.

I lowered my eyes first and mumbled an apology. Immaculate, still pinned under him, said: 'Leave the boy alone, Peter.'

'He's my brother,' Peter said.

And he removed the blanket that covered them. The heavy lead of my mind sank quickly into my belly. I stared. Then, like a drunk in a daze, I got up, knocked a chair over and tottered towards the door. Before I knew what I was doing I was gleefully

40

talking to myself over a beer in an African night-club some five miles away.

She finally tracked me down late that night and found me raving blind drunk. I woke up in some bed in the small hours and there was someone asleep in my arms. I lit a match. It flared for an instant upon Immaculate's sleeping face. A blue-grey spider lay on her exposed cheek. But when I held the match closer there was nothing there, nothing but the faint outlines of a dimple.

The match went out. The shadows closed around us with a noiseless cosmic violence. It woke her up. Her voice had an inner light stirring within it; the way clouds seem to have in their heart a trembling clarity. She spoke of many things, and fragments of things. She spoke with an intensity that seemed to refract my character the way a prism analyses clearly the light striking its surfaces. That I have no recollection of what it was she spoke about reveals much of the dirtier side of my nature. But I in turn told her about my nervous breakdown when I had become aware of persons around me whom no one else could see. They could not have been the black heroes whom I sought – or perhaps they were. I don't know. There had been four of them; three men in threadbare clothes and the woman of the faded shawl. This had happened a few weeks before my sixth form examinations – which I then had to write with the assistance of a massive dose of white tranquillisers and pink triangular pills. At first the three men and the woman merely followed me about the school saying nothing but just being *there*. Crudely there. I would be talking to friends and then become intensely aware of *them* standing close to my friends. I would be in the history classroom listening to the history master and as usual taking notes and things when I would with a leap of the heartbeat realise that *they* were in the room, moving about, following the teacher, sitting down when he sat, and aping his every gesture. Or after our football practice when we were in the showers *they* would appear standing stiffly watching my nakedness. One day this so terrified me that I rushed stark naked out of the showers screaming my head off. Their attacks after that became more mischievous. They began to *talk*. I could hear them talking compulsively – even when I could not see them. My friends heard nothing, but I began to suspect everyone of trying to undermine my reason. I became rather impossible, and the psychiatrist said I must only attend classes when I 'felt like it.' I began to spend more time in the art studio, where I discovered to my consternation that I could not paint anything which did not have something sinister in it. Meanwhile the voices continued to torment me; growing not only in intensity but also in their outrageousness. I never told the psychiatrist the whole truth about what the voices were *saying*; but I did send off a series of hysterical missives to Peter demanding 'the truth of the matter'. He did not even bother to answer them. (I have a good mind to publish those strange letters right now.) What the voices said was something quite obscene about my mother's morals; and every day I writhed in agony over this bed of glowing coals. The air reeked of guilt. And shame. And outrage. And scandal. Mountains of argument ranged through my mind until the earthquake of those infernal voices brought them crushing down upon my toes. The absurd, the grotesque, it seemed, had come home to stay. Where are the bloody heroes? My fear of heights had not restrained me from climbing the cliffs of my nerves. And the demons, finding the House unattended, had calmly strutted in through the open door. Had I been a good atheist, perhaps ... The voices took out of my suitcase every little wrong I had done and derisively exhibited it before my eyes. Every evil thought – from lechery to vanity – was held up before my eyes, and I felt like a slimy worm. The objects, smells and presences around me seemed to contain at the centre of their lens the sharp details of those little teeth that were biting into my mind. I opened my mouth to give my defence plea but the voices had not only found me out, they had also taken over the inner chords of my own voice. I talked compulsively. My voice seemed to be contained by the refracting lattices of transparent stones. Little thrusts of swift lights, diamond sparks, spinning maddeningly, leaped through my mind until I could not bear the headache of it. My condition deteriorated: severe palpitations set in and I made it worse by reading all about heart disease in the *Encyclopaedia Britannica.* And I was cold; I have never been so cold in my life. The ice of it singed my very thoughts; my voice was breaking and the unusual sound of it made me jump irritably. It seemed to me something was taking over my body; the images and symbols I had for so long taken for granted had taken upon themselves a strange hue; and I was losing my grasp of simple speech. I began to ramble, incoherently, in a disconnected manner. I was being severed from my own voice. I would listen to it as to a still, small voice coming from the huge distances of the mind. It was like this: English is my second language, Shona my first. When I talked it was in the form of an interminable argument, one side of which was always expressed in English and the other side always in Shona. At the same time I would be aware of myself as something indistinct but separate from both cultures. I felt gagged by this absurd contest between Shona and English. I knew no other language: my French and Latin were enough to make me wary of conversing in them. However some nights I could feel the French and the Latin fighting it out in the shadowy background of the English and Shona. The fights completely muzzled me. The conversation, the arguments and pleas steadily asserted their own independence; and I wandered about drugged to the hilt by tranquillisers and feeling literally robbed of words. That is when *they* began to laugh. Their laughter was of the crudest type, obscene. It reduced my whole world to a turd. Its stench got into my food, my painting, my reading and my dreams. Everything I touched turned into a stinking horror. Julia alone

43

made it possible for me to survive that impish laughter. Everyone at the school knew I had become a 'loony' and occasionally some of the boys, especially Harry, would play tricks on me. At one point these cruel tricks drove me out of the dormitory altogether and I was given a room at the priory where of course I accused everyone of trying to poison me. Julia, though rather maddening in those days, was the only reason for living. She knew so much more about sex that sometimes I feared for my soul.

Then one afternoon the sun had rings around it. Its light was at once sickly and remote; a sure sign that the rains were coming. That night – we were at prep; it must have been about nine-thirty – a great charge of lightning exploded, striking the humid air with a sinister violence. At once massive rocks of rain hurled themselves down upon the sleeping earth. The noise was deafening to the ear, the sight awesome to the eye, and the great torrents almost startled me into premature senility. Such a madness of the elements did not seem possible. Rude buckets of water poured over the school. It rained as though it would flood us out of our minds. It drummed on the asbestos roofs. It drummed on the window-panes. It dinned into our minds. It drummed down upon us until we could not stand it. It poured darkly; plashed; guttered; broke down upon our heads like the smack of a fist. It roared, splashed, soaked, stuttered stertorously down from the black spaces of the huge mindless universe. It rose. It swelled. It cracked its sides like a whip. Silver fish seemed to leap in frenzy by the bucketful. The mud plash and sucking of it churned round and round in our minds. It chilled up to the shoulders of one's soul. The delirium of rain shook the school into a feverish excitement. The eruption was like a boil that bursts and splatters everything with its black acids. The angry skies drove boulders of rain against the school until we felt our very sanity was under a relentless siege. The singing fury of it stuck little needles into the matter of our brains. It boomed. It dammed up.

It welled. It roared the lions out of voice. It spilled down into our minds, soaked our words, and left us openmouthed. Mouthwet. The air reeked of nothing else. Its sweet evil tang stuck like glue to our clothes. Things floated in it and they were our former assurance. At the cemetery the cheaper graves were gutted with it and the little wooden stakes and crosses were swept away. A drunken teacher who recklessly dared it was never seen again. That rain, it knocked more than the breath out of you. That rain, it drummed the drum until the drum burst, stitching the mind with thongs of lightning. It was like a madman talking incessantly; whispering rapidly into the ear of the sky. It was like a man who, suddenly bereaved, breaks down and hurls himself at the wall. It was a great river plunging over a falls and roaring the cerebral rage that can only be broken by the rocks below. The rain, it broke down the workers' compound; it felled the huts with its brute knuckle- duster. It knocked down the mud walls and brought the flimsy roofs crushing down upon the unlucky occupants. All over the compound men, women and children fought for their homes that night, building, rebuilding, groaning against its blows until once again the walls of that malice came crushing down. And still the skies dribbled compulsively upon the earth. That rain: it chattered its sharp little teeth; it foamed at the mouth against everything. The argument of it left us stunned. The words hit us again and again with each bucketful of rain. Something diseased had been unleashed among us. Its inflammation seared like a flash of pain, a bolt of intuition beating the madness out of me. It cracked the skin of our teeth. My seed-bed was utterly wrecked; there was in the rain the swollen seeds of an old feud; its raw smell had reached down into the secrets of the earth's lungs. Its muddy feet had trampled and stained everything I held dear. It soaked the memory. It held the only sun of former days prisoner to its lusts. And the colours of the mind began to run down the canvas until everything had ruined everything else. No sooner

45

had I listened to it for what seemed five seconds – but was really twenty-five minutes, because the bell rang to end the prep period – than I realised that I could not move from my chair. I was so frightened of the prospect of running through that malign storm that I was quite prepared to stay the night in my cubicle. Harry, whose cubicle was next to mine, began to sing tragically:

> Shure kwehure kunotambatamba haaa!
> Shure kwehure kunotambatamba haaa!
> Kanandazofa ndinokuchengetera nzvimbo haa!
> Kanandazofa ndinokuchengetera nzvimbo haa!

People were moving about the room. Edmund farted and Stephen shouted something about Kwame Nkrumah. The girls had already gone. Most of the boys soon left. Something fell on to the open pages of my book; I choked back my scream when I realised what it was and swivelled round in anger. Tricks again! Harry was laughing sympathetically.

'It won't tempt you. 'It's not real, man,' Harry said.

And he reached forward to retrieve his rubber snake.

I was too mad for words. I had struck him down in an instant and before I knew what I was at I had smashed my chair over his back, once, twice. I flung the chair away and, more frightened at what was changing inside me than whether Harry was all right, looked out into the clashes of light, out there in the storm, flickering through my mind. I think I knew then what was in store for me. But I felt elated, as though the worst had already been. This was an illusion – and yet a step in the right direction. Something resolute. Something sure. As I read it, lightning stabbed the air and as it thundered I swung round quickly enough to dodge most of the blow of the chair which Harry had flung at my head. The blow knocked me sideways. Before I could recover, Harry had dashed out into the storm. I was after him in an instant – picking up the rubber snake and stuffing it into my pocket. The storm grabbed me around the body and hurled me after Harry. Utter blackness alternated with flickerings of eel-like lightning. The rocks of rain had immediately drenched me to the marrow. And then something jumped upon my back and I fell face flat in the churning mud of the night. Something was trampling me into the sticky mess of mud. I grabbed for a leg and twisted. Harry cursed as he fell. And then we went for each other like madmen. But neither gained any advantage. We fought and plastered ourselves with mud and blood while the massive rocks of rain hurled themselves down upon our bare heads. We fought until we were so tired that our blows could not have flattened ice-cream; indeed, our blows seemed like a lover's teasing and our struggles had become embraces. Our kicks were mere coquetry. And then something supremely white, blindingly so, erupted at the heart of the storm, striking us down in a heap in all that mud. I began to laugh. Harry began to laugh. We were both as helpless as if the laughter was the final say of the storm. It was a new clarity – the kind of madness that overcomes Pauline travellers on the road to Damascus. We shed our clothes as we laughed and began to paint each other's bodies with handfuls of mud. Earth to earth. We were so engrossed in this that we did not notice that not only were we standing in the middle of the gravel road but also a car with its headlights full upon us had stopped and its driver was blaring his horn repeatedly. We must have looked worse than ghosts. It was Harry's idea to scare the poor chap out of his wits; which we did only too well. He was our history master, and he never recovered from the experience. He began to have fits; and had to be replaced because they found him one night raving on the roof of his house and shouting that he was Elijah the Prophet. When Harry and I returned to the dormitories we went to the showers and there the miracle happened – I almost cried with glee. *They* had gone! I could feel it. They had erased themselves into the invisible airs of the storm. The daemon had been exorcised and gone into the Gadarene swine. For the first time in my life I felt completely alone. Totally on my own. It is as if a storm should rage in one's mind and no one else has the faintest experience of it. It frightened me a little. I was learning to keep my claws sheathed.

'What do you make of it?' I asked.

She said nothing.

She had fallen asleep while I was telling her about it.

Her father was a priest in the Roman Catholic Church. But fortune had not always smiled on him. He had started life just like any other half-starved homeless vagrant. A 'lucky' chance – an encounter with a racist but benevolent white priest – pushed his foot up on to the first rung: he became a catechist, bullying old and young alike and accusing women – those who repulsed his advances – of witchcraft and sorcery. He won his Standard Six certificate, and soon afterwards became a deacon and then a priest. What more could a man want? A wife and children – that he already had. And from chimney to pulpit he began to denounce all African customs; from desk to dustbin he carted out all manner of filthy traditions which in reality were the only strengths still in the minds of his own people. And then when Immaculate – it was he who gave her that ridiculous name – became pregnant, he became like a fierce bull that is conscious of being trifled with by a ninny of a matador. He saw red; and with one dust-snuffling toss of his massive horns he cast her out. From then on he turned his attention to politics – and to Harry. He came to address our sixth form twice and on both occasions found reason to rebuke my disrespect for the cloth: the second time was during my nervous breakdown, when I shouted 'It's people like you who're driving us mad!' I wanted to say more, but I began to stammer and he took advantage of that to say 'It's the ape in you, young man, the heart of darkness.'

He went on: 'Humility is the gateway to the halls of government. The humility I mean is this: you had nothing but the ape-man in you. Then Jesus Christ came ...?'

My inkwell missed his head by a breath and smashed into the wall behind him.

But he shouted all the louder: 'You had nothing but the ape-grin in your brains. And the white man came. Look around you. Surely the industry and progress ...'

A large lump of sadza hit him squarely in the face. But he seemed to draw strength from it and to drag it full-blast out of his lungs of the earth: 'Render unto Caesar the things that are Caesar's. St Paul himself, in ...'

Three lumps of sadza flung from different points of the room scored direct hits on his grey head.

But with a resolute shake of his stooping shoulders he cried out triumphantly: '... in the Epistle to the Romans it specifically says that loyalty rather than insurrection is the supreme Christian virtue.'

There was dead silence as he lowered his voice dramatically and continued in a more confidential tone: 'I was also, like you, restless and impatient. Listen, I never had the chance – which you have now – of a formal education. My youth was a hungry and impatient one; but my hunger was not for the things of this world. My impatience was for the coming of a greater reality. Those of you who know me well know that I was a homeless orphan: without shelter, without food, without a father, without a mother, without brothers or sisters, without the comfort of friends. There was a great void in my heart. That vast emptiness was the horror of the heart of darkness.'

('The horror – the horror!' Edmund mimicked unconvincingly. Joseph Conrad was one of our set authors then.)

At this point the door was flung open and Father Johnson entered in great agitation. He took one look at our handiwork (the ink, the mess of sadza) and as usual looked so shocked that no one dared breathe lest our breath knocked him down. Finally he took the priest by the arm and led him out of the room. As the door closed gently behind them Edmund whispered loudly 'Ready, steady, go!' and the room resounded with catcalls, hoots, howls, ululations, screeches, whistles and the mind-bending agony of tables being drummed black and blue.

'Bloody missionaries!'

'Bloody whites!'

'They had the Bible!'

'We had the land!'

'Now they have the land!'

'And we have the Bible!'

'Bloody sell-outs!'

(Harry looked as though he had just been swallowed alive by Jonah's whale.)

'And what about Tangwena!'

'And where is Nkomo!'

'Sithole!'

'Magandanga edau!'

(Harry in confusion had within the whale begun to sing loudly and discordantly:

Shure kwehure kunotambatamba haa!

Shure kwehure kunotambatamba haaa!

Kanandazofa ndinokuchengetera nzvimbo!)

Someone mistook Harry's song for a political one; and began to join in with:

Tsuro tsuro woye ndapera basa!

Tsuro tsuro woye naNkomo!

I do not quite know what happened next. Something seemed to split my mind open. The floor rushed rapidly upwards to meet me; out of the corner of my eye I saw Harry rushing anxiously towards me. I opened my mouth to say something. There was this dark pit. I was falling gently into it. A tiny star erupted and the flying sparks of its minute explosion and the overpowering smell of blood woke me hours later. My head seemed encased in a fiendish ice-hold; but when I explored with my hand, ripping off the bandages and feeling around the wet stinging wound, it was only the cold cold stitches they had used on the gash. Stitches enough to weave webs from the one wall of my mind to the wall of the House of Hunger.

And the mind slowly became the room. And the room – floor, roof, walls – was boxed in by other rooms. There were posters on the walls; faded posters peeling off the egg-cracks in the walls of my mind. Of the room. One said Earth. One said Fire. One said Water. One said Air. One said I am Stone. And they were all contained within each other, papering over the cracks. Another was a bushman painting: a series of lines tracing out exactly the instant of the killing of a gazelle. The inner lens of the artist had captured in those few deft lines the incredible face of human existence. Another was a toothy photograph of a black man, ankle over knee, grinning, holding in each hand a cheap cigar and a rolled cigarette. A price-tag pinned to his cheek read: 'Fugard'. A tiny badge like a star on his cream lapel punched upwards leaping into my magnifying lens; it screamed quietly 'I AM ME'. The gold pin on his pastel tie depicted the private parts of a bisexual being.

The ceiling was pasted over with the crinkled fragments of a sky that had been cut up recklessly with an old razor. In the centre of them, written in minute letters the colour of dawn, was the legend CIVILISATION. But some enterprising vandal had scrawled over it the two words BLACK IS.

51

The floor was a mirror reflecting in reverse the parable of the ceiling. The same vandal – possibly Edmund – had painted on it in red letters: ART IS FART.

I had only been in the room for a few seconds when I began to hear the tiny maddening sound. I shifted my weight, listening. It was the sound of distant footsteps coming and going in all the other rooms that pressed against my room. Feet exactly taking step in time with each other; coming and going. Trudging and turning just behind a point midway between my eyes.

There was this window.

I walked towards it and stuck my head out.

There were thousands of windows out there and there were heads sticking out of them. Heads black like me.

I drew back staring at the window itself.

It was a mirror.

I stuck my head out through it again.

Thousands of black heads were sticking out of thousands of windows.

A tiny explosion erupted and streaked through my head like the sparking trail of a falling star. It multiplied into millions of glowing fireflies.

Flame-lilies.

Something fighting floated down from a pale blue sky. As it floated down to my level I saw that it was a black man and a white man locked in the embraces of struggle.

A split second later the thing splintered into the room, knocking me clear across the floor. The fighting thing exploded into a tremendous din, sparks flying.

The heat sucked the oxygen out of my brain.

The blow rang angrily, roaring in my ears.

I looked.

The thing was gone.

But there was on the floor a star cut out of toilet paper.

Soft toilet paper.

I groped towards it and blew.

Ppfffphhp.

It flew upwards. It hovered unsteadily. It floundered. It sailed straight for the window. On its underside was written the legend ZIMBABWE.

Those black heroes ...

I stuck my head out of the window.

The star shot upwards until it was no more than a glint upon the retina of the sky.

Somewhere a toilet flushed; and drowned the room.

My thoughts chalked themselves on the black page of a dreamless sleep. In the morning there was not a single space left on that page: the story was complete. As I read it every single word erased itself into my mind. Afterwards they came to take out the stitches from the wound of it. And I was whole again. The stitches were published. The reviewers made obscene noises. It is now out of print.

But those stitches, those poems ...

The sunlight singled out the grim dirt that had formed on the whitewashed wall. Flies buzzed out hallelujahs. A furry spider drew in its eight legs and studied me cautiously. A chameleon etched delicately against the stains of dirt on the wall, sucked its lips and swivelled its old eye towards the pimple on my cheek. A wisp of cloud drifting contentedly across the sun cast upon me a whimsical shadow of a look. The variegated weeds at my feet conversed gently to and fro, pausing again to chide my clumsy shoes. A floating seed rocked itself quizzically on my scarred wrist and, dissatisfied, slowly took off into the air. A crow hovered in mid-flight and slowly contemplated the top of my head; a liquid bomb plashing on my prematurely grey hair was that sage's assessment of my character ...

But those stitches ...

A heap of soiled dishes scolded and squabbled on the grease-strewn table. An unruly crowd of empty beer-bottles had gathered in the shadows of the grimy wash-basin. The robot cupboard had exposed its privates: a troop of salt and pepper tins reinforced by a bloody ketchup character whose ominous look drove me hurriedly into the bathroom.

The toilet bowl did not flinch when I sat on him. The paper protested crisply but I did not show any mercy. When I shook his arm gratefully he flushed, roaring immovably as I pulled up my sullen trousers.

Yes, those stitches, those poems ...

The grains of the gravel walk gritted their teeth beneath my clumsy shoes. The night sky squinted through its lunar monocle and leaned over to regard the eclipse of my iron soul. A cold breath of air blew gently against the back of my neck and whispered inaudibly of skulls staring upwards through six feet of dirt.

The pane misted soothingly against my lips. I could see in the Great Hall thousands of heads opening and shutting against great glasses of secretive beer. On the platform were five heads; one was opening and shutting against an offended microphone. Three were furiously scratching the bellies of itchy guitars. The fifth head, tightly locked within itself, was butting against the stretched skin of drums that no longer knew pain. In the space directly beneath the platform there was a scarred head dancing clumsily with a haughty chair.

These, too, were the stitches.

How many sheep did you wear last winter?

Those who have climbed the highest Everest of pain have stuck their flag upon it. The rest of us may as well –

'Publish the stitches?'

'No.'

The stitches run like the great dyke across the country. A

little blood still seeps through; it is like red ink on a child's teeth. The bloodstains on my plate accuse the appetite that goes into eating. The stains on the sheet when she left the next morning refused to be laundered away. In the sky, God's stains are beautiful to see from down below or from up above.

Those who eat brains only ...

'Fuck!' Julia exploded.

'What's wrong now?' I asked, feigning innocence.

'You.'

'Sorry.'

She snorted. Her painted fingernails gleamed like claws around her cigarette. She was probably thinking I would be easy prey; it saddened me a little to think that she had become one of those persons who depend for their sanity solely on the measure of their claws. The measure of the stains left behind. Stains! The barman, impressed by her massive breasts, was thoughtfully reducing her to a stain on a sheet. A true hero of our time. Reducing everything to shit.

'What is Philip doing now?' she asked.

'Advertising. He's thinking of switching to RTV.'

She was staring. I knew what was coming. Drink affected her that way. The way she stared – I looked hastily to see if my fly was open. It wasn't. I said: 'There was this magazine Philip and I were going to bring out. Poetry and short stories. We wanted to do something of what Lermontov did. Two chaps, Doug and Citre, who worked with him, were going to join us. White youngsters. But Doug got busted for drugs. Citre fled the country to escape the military dragnet. And my uncle turned me out of the house because the police kept checking up on me. The magazine never materialised. And Philip was lucky not to get the sack.'

I stopped.

She was still dissecting me with her oblique scalpel look

A glass of clear water, knocked sideways, and frozen in mid-toppling: that's how I felt.

I went on rather desperately: 'It was a bad patch for Philip. I was just getting into dagga. And liking it. Of course he did not fully trust me any more because of a certain woman. I mean he kept talking in parables about a certain Judas figure. The chap who betrayed Troy. Incanor, was it? Imagine the human body having within itself a built-in Trojan Horse. And saying there was nothing finer in the world than the figures on a Greek vase. Ode to a Grecian Urn and all that. All rot, of course. But our meetings were like that. It was the dagga, I suppose. Boredom had lit up our brains. That there is a divine spark in a human being, however low. The limitations of reason. And something about the Yahoos and those horses. Do you remember Lobengula's letter to the Queen? "Some time ago a party of men came into my country, the principal being a man named Rudd. They asked me for a place to dig gold and said that they would give me certain things for the right to do so. I told them to bring what they would give, and I would show them what I would give. A document was written and presented to me for signature. I asked what it contained, and was told that in it were my words and the words of those men. I put my hand to it. About three months afterwards I heard from other sources that I had given, by that document, the right to all the minerals in my country. I called a meeting of my indunas, and also of the white men, and demanded a copy of that document. It was proved to me that I had signed away the mineral rights of my whole country to Rudd and his friends." Poor chap. I don't like to blame him though, for making us all like this. Of course he was rather silly. Poking his head into a Pandora's box. Deserved what he got. Like a baboon poking his hand into a gourd-trap. Of course you and I would be amahole, slaves, if the poor chap had survived. Chief Moghabi refused to submit to authority and was killed. Chief Ngomo did the same and he and his people were killed with a seven-pounder and a Maxim gun. We did not,

I suppose, want to be slaves of either the heroic Ndebele or the Lendy–Jameson gang. Jameson said: "Mashonas are servants of white men." Mtshete said: "To whom do the Mashona belong if they do not belong to the king?" Of course the understatement of the year came from Lobengula, who said of white men: "You people must want something from me."

'And then,' I said, 'war. Of a sort. The Maxim and other guns began to speak and within a quarter of an hour the surrounding country was strewn with dead and wounded. This was at Shangani. At Mbembezi the Maxims also spoke; within half an hour a thousand Ndebele had fallen. Lobengula fled Bulawayo. And after crossing the Shangani admitted defeat. He said: "They have beaten my regiments, killed my people, burnt my kraals, captured my cattle, and I want peace." The one thing that bugs me about the man is that he even loved white men. That he killed my people like cattle, the way Germans killed Jews. And he loved white men. Even trusted them. And then he wanted to know if Queen Victoria really existed. Wives and all that. What I mean is: is this all there is to our history? There is a stinking deceit at the heart of it. Petty intrigues. White hoboes. Bloody missionaries singing Onward Christian Soldiers. Where are the bloody heroes? Do you remember the words of that dying warrior at Mbembezi: "Wau! To think the Imbezu regiments were defeated by a lot of beardless boys!" After all, even the goddamn Rudd concession almost got lost in the Kalahari desert when that chap got lost in it and all he had was gold and champagne and brandy and stout: and when he couldn't hope any more he buried the blasted concession in, of all places, an ant-bear hole and the stupid Bushmen helped him, and so here we are all sticky with the stinking stains of history. Smouldering and farting ...'

I paused because there were glittering gems crystallising out of the brine of her large clear eyes. And a stiffening of limbs. Those are pearls that were his eyes, said Shakespeare. Pearls are the lucid translation of agony into refracting lattices. I could not stand the light of them. I shook my head – my mind was now just a cloud of alcohol. No wonder I was rambling like this. What, with an education like ...

'Some bastard,' I said, 'some bastard beat up Philip's sister. Anne, that's her name, she was beaten black and blue. Raped her out of her mind too. But we found him – I did. He thought he could skulk behind Nestar's skirts. But I found him. And phoned Philip, who crunched into him the way a pickaxe smacks into a wedding cake.'

Julia smiled a tiny star.

'How can a black person be beaten black and blue?' she demanded.

She had latched on to the one subject with which she could browbeat me the way a cruel boy once tormented Lucius the Golden Ass by beating him on the same spot. The same inflamed raw spot – beating Lucius there with a great stick.

'It's just an expression,' I said wearily.

She did not want to know about Anne. One learns a lot about people by merely studying what they do not want to know. Everybody doesn't want to know something or other. I did not want to know what I really felt about mother, about Immaculate. And about – but Julia was getting on to that.

'It's not,' she retorted. 'You are awfully mixed up.'

Most educated Africans like the word 'awfully', the word 'actually', the phrase 'Is it not?' They are the open-sesame to success. Actually, class-consciousness and the conservative snobbery that goes with it are deeply rooted in the African elite, who are in the same breath able to shout LIBERATION, POLYGAMY without feeling that something is unhinged. It's awfully trying. I have, of course, my own pet words and allusions which reveal to the eager listener just what kind of a bastard I am. Harry has got style; I too have got ... But Julia was already unwrapping the ghastly business.

'I know,' I said quickly.

'No, you don't know. It's the way you ... talk sometimes. Your moods. And the way you never actually seem to look at things.'

Her painted claws reached out and closed over my fist. The hyena, the wild dog, the vulture had finally seen that I could not defend myself because the lions before her had already picked my bones clean. I have always wondered how people *know* that their victim has been cowed enough to submit to being eaten. They know intuitively, instinctively, Stephen once said as he licked his chops over Edmund's physical weakness. Lobengula finally agreed to be eaten by Rhodes. My generation had all but been consumed by gut-rot; it is as if there was a tiny drill burring inside one's brains. Now masturbation –

Her sharp little teeth gleamed. Something tiny erupted in the sky of her eyes.

'You hate being black,' she said.

My discoloured teeth ached. Here we go again, I thought. Can a hollow decayed soul be filled in, the way dentists do it to a mess of teeth? Did she want me to flaunt my horns and hooves? If teething is natural in babies, why not in new wine? Harry's toothpaste character. Me and my dentures. Lightning stitching the air.

I swallowed. My voice had become rather hoarse. My gums were aching as if the Second Coming was around the corner, after more than eighty years of gut-rot.

'Take a close look at me,' I said, 'And then see if you can repeat what you've just said.'

She took a long detailed look at my incredible face.

And she burst out laughing.

My voice grew small and remote, the way it does when impotent anger spreads and paralyses my faculty for logical thought. I talked rapidly in that small-toothed voice. I could feel inside my head a fine handsaw gnawing swiftly, gnawing maddeningly. And something was twitching in the barman's face. And, outside, thousands of flies, whipped up into a frenzy by their invisible conductor, buzzed a crescendo of Handel's 'Hallelujah Chorus', while the thin sunlight-foil glinted and flashed with the crinkled delight of it all.

– The old man died beneath the wheels of the twentieth century. There was nothing left but stains, bloodstains and fragments of flesh, when the whole length of it was through with eating him. And the same thing is happening to my generation. No, I don't hate being black. I'm just tired of saying it's beautiful. No, I don't hate myself. I'm just tired of people bruising their knuckles on my jaw. I'm tired of racking my brains in the doorway. I don't know. Nothing turns out as exactly intended. A cruel sarcasm rules our lives. Sometimes freedom's opportunity is a wide waistline. The bulldozers have been and gone and where once our heroes danced there is nothing but a hideous stain. They stretched the wings of our race, stretched them out against the candle-flame. There was nothing left but the genitals of senile gods. My life – my life is a spider's web; it is studded with minute skeletons of genius – My life –

'Oh shit!' she muttered, as though she had forgotten something.

'My life ...'

I was sweating from the rush of words.

She deftly licked the rim of her glass with a quick red tongue. 'You don't have to take that line with me,' she said.

I took a deep breath.

'You like to worry my old sore, don't you?' I asked.

'To bring you out of yourself,' she said.

'There's nothing to bring out.'

Her nails dug into my wrist.

60

'There's always the old semen,' she said.

Once more my cheeks – though more slowly this time – sank into my boots. I held my breath.

'Tubes,' she said. 'That's what being human means. Insides. Entrails. All twisted up in a knot. A red knot.'

'The augury of life-steaming entrails,' I mumbled.

'When I was young,' she said, 'I wanted to look at my insides. Rip them inside out and see what I really was like.'

I had retreated behind my drink.

'How is the old lubrication?' she persisted.

'Weird.'

'Today I woke up feeling all me,' she said.

Something stirred in my nether regions, turning her into a mere receptacle for the stains that had made everything nasty.

'I'm still feeling that way,' she said. 'I could do one more of those films with that chap – what was his name – he screwed very well, as though he was drawing circles with his loins. What was his name?'

'Citre.'

'Do you think white girls are any better in bed? That Patricia, for instance.'

'The weather was rather humid. Sort of sticky and stuffy, you couldn't keep it in without slipping and falling to the rocks below.'

She looked shocked. 'I didn't quite catch that,' she said.

'It must have been crushed on the rocks then.'

The claws relaxed their grip on my wrist. But she put on her armour again and with the speed of greased lightning promptly dispatched Hector: 'You wrote verses to Patricia, didn't you? The way you two carried on you'd think ...'

'All right, all right. I plead guilty to every charge you're going to move against me. And what's more, I still think a lot about her.'

'The campus was up to its ears about your sordid goings on,' she said. 'How did you reconcile your politics with your sexual adventures?'

I sighed.

'I admit there were certain persons who made certain derogatory remarks about it. For instance, Harry ...'

'What?'

'He said she looked like the back of a bus and he wanted to know how on earth I mounted it.'

Once more my cheeks were gradually creeping up my legs and my trunk.

'But what's the point of all this, Julia?'

She said nothing.

'I mean, you ought to know me better than that.'

She gritted her small sharp teeth and the sound made me wince. I knew that the moment had come to keep my mouth shut. I closed my eyes and watched the curtained insides of my eyelids. But the voice persisted: 'You disgust me!'

A spot of her spittled words stung into my left cheek. A tiny star collapsed into itself in my chest. When I coughed I had to swallow a lot of phlegm. The pain of it dragged my cheeks back into my face.

She shifted her chair so that no one but me could see what she was doing. Her hand, those painted claws, had closed tightly around my privates. I decided there and then that enough was enough. In a deliberately loud voice, so that heads turned, I said: 'Julia, take your hand off my penis!'

When I was four years old I used to sleep in the cramped space between the wall and my parents' bed. And eight nights a week the maniacal symphonies of their screwing dinned into my mind. Then for one whole week father did not come home and I slept in the bed with mother. The following week father had still not come home. One night I had just about drifted off to sleep when I woke up screaming that there was a man at the window. But she hushed me and opened the window and let him in. He instantly jumped into the bed on top of her while I reluctantly eased down on to the cold cement floor. Soon there were tremendous groans and grunts erupting from that bed and the energy of it was like god's fist shaking satan's shirtfront. The avalanche of it was even enough to wake Peter, who usually slept like a boa constrictor that has swallowed an elephant. He at a glance sized up the situation; like a bat out of hell he flung himself at the man who, however – without even pausing in his screwing of mother – knocked him out cold with a backhander. Father came back three days later. I said nothing. Peter grimly said nothing. And mother looked like she was not thinking about anything at all.

My street education was no less explicit. The advent of pubic hairs and unmanly breasts (you were supposed to squeeze them, or to pick up an angry ant and let it bite the nipple) was brought to my gang quite graphically by Peter. He was the first to have pubic hairs worth exposing. He was the first to actually induce Nestar to take down her knickers and bend over. And one thick summer night the boys came from all over the township and gathered round to watch a demonstration Peter had promised. He was going to prove to us infants that he had actually become capable of making girls – any girls – pregnant. It was a solemn occasion. We were going to see the thing that divided the men from the boys. Peter stripped. He had bathed and oiled himself all over. He was lean and strong and handsome. The size of his organ astonished us. It was stiff and huge and its mouth was tense. He quite casually cradled it in his right-hand fingers and began to masturbate. We watched him with mounting eagerness. Above us white termites flashed and spurted about the naked light bulb of the solitary street-light. I began to sweat. He groaned, and – moved. He was losing control. We could see a great happening taking over his soul. It was in his spine, arching him backward, and yet lifting him – gradually. It was as if he stood between two magnets, and the iron filings of his nerves were being tortured into a pattern. The taut cloth of his being, unable to bear the strain, tore. And, moaning like something out of this world, he came and came and came like new wine that cannot be contained within old cloth. The gang drew closer and closer and sighed. I swallowed thickly, but my mouth was dry. And my mouth, it seems, has been dry ever since.

These discoveries made us bolder. There was in the township a large floating population of prostitutes. (Nestar was to become a queen among them.) Most of them had nowhere secret to take their numerous clients. They used the bush instead. The countryside, up to then, had left me cold and indifferent; later a hasty affair with Wordsworth's *Prelude* swung me to the opposite extreme. Anyway, I and the gang used to take our lives into our hands and follow the prostitutes and their clients into the heart of the bush, where it seemed the heart of the matter was daily revealing itself to the world. I did have a good pair of running legs and could jump over or through thorn hedges. One day we followed a woman back into the township. There was nothing particularly interesting about her. It's just that we could see on the gravel road splotches and stains of semen that were dripping down her as she walked. Years later I was to write a story using her as a symbol of Rhodesia.

The girls were also learning. Once every month a girl would be expelled from the school because she had become pregnant. One of them – Nestar – caused me much discouragement. She got pregnant, was cast out of school and home and church and is now one of the most famous whores in the whole country.

The older generation too was learning. It still believed that if one did not beat up one's wife it meant that one did not love her at all. These beatings (not entirely one-sided, because the man next door tried it and was smashed into the Africans Only hospital by his up to then submissive wife) were always salted and peppered by the outrageous statements of the participants about the morals of either party. The most lively of them ended with the husband actually fucking – raping – his wife right there in the thick of the excited crowd. He was cursing all women to hell as he did so. And he seemed to screw her forever – he went on and on and on and on until she looked like death. When at last – the crowd licked its lips and swallowed – when at last he pulled his penis out of her raw thing and stuffed it back into his trousers, I think she seemed to move a finger, which made us all wonder how she could have survived such a determined assault.

But the best lessons we had in hardihood were not from the example of the males. There were more male than female lunatics; more male than female beggars; more male than female alcoholics ... And they seemed to know that the upraised black fist of power would fill up more lunatic asylums than it would swell the numbers of our political martyrs. And when the Pill fell like manna from God's bounty –

But the young woman's life is not at all an easy one; the black young woman's. She is bombarded daily by a TV network that assumes that black women are not only ugly but also they do not exist unless they take in laundry, scrub lavatories, polish staircases, and drudge around in a nanny's uniform. She is mugged every day by magazines that pressure her into buying European beauty; and the advice columns have such nuggets like 'Understanding is the best thing in the world, therefore be more cheerful when he comes home looking like thunder.' And the only time the *Herald* mentions her is when she has – in 1896/7 – led an uprising against the State and been safely cheered by the firing squad or when she is caught for the umpteenth time soliciting in Vice Mile.

When Nestar (what kind of a father would give his child a

name like that?) was cast out she knew nothing about survival in the streets. The married man who had made her pregnant beat her up when she went to him for help. She was twelve then. She slept in waiting rooms and lavatories at the bus station and at the railway station. I don't know what she ate to keep herself going. Later when I asked her if she had thought of suicide she almost bit my head off.

'Suicide!' she scoffed. 'That's for educated lunatics like you.'

She gave birth to a son in the bush. When I later asked her where she said abstractedly: 'At the head of the stream. There was blood everywhere but he looked like a new smooth stone when I washed him.'

I did not want to talk about him because of what Philip and I were going to do to him.

The pain, blood and emptiness of that birth made her there and then decide to 'fight into the thick of the money'. Money, she said, was power. There is nothing worthwhile that has no gold in it, she said.

I looked round the room: she had certainly found the pot of gold and stolen it from the Rainbow-serpent.

'White men have a thing about black women, you know,' she confided. 'And there was nothing I wouldn't do. Most wouldn't even touch me. They'd just make me do things and they'd watch with their eyeballs sticking out. And masturbate like hell. But there was one who always had the same old thing. I would suck his balls and he would come off into my hair. He would really grease my hair with the stuff. Rubbing it in like a bishop laying on hands, while I licked the rest of the drops from his stick. Then he would make me stick my arse right out into the sky of his face with my head between my knees and he would breathe it in like god accepting incense and then the baptism would come when he'd sort of writhe and cry for me to fart and urinate into his face.

Like rain. A sort of storm scene. And then there was Billy.'

She wrinkled her brow with the effort to remember.

My writing pad was on the fur rug: I had long stopped taking notes.

She went on.

'Billy knew all there was to know about orgasms. He'd simply explode into a long hysterical one just at the sight of my body. And he couldn't stick it in enough. He'd sort of crumble up like a biscuit and cry as though he just couldn't believe it. And he always called me Mother. He'd just tense up. And slowly break up like the little dry twig of God's still, small voice. And swearing with glee like a schoolboy. He liked to fuck me to the sound of Shostakovitch's *Leningrad Symphony*.'

She paused to look at the expensive rings on her fingers. I looked around the room. An elegant TV nestled in the corner, by a marble statue of Venus. A bowl of apples – like a discreet symbol – nested on a lovely pastel patchwork. My clumsy shoes were safely hidden in the thick rich carpet. And on the wall facing me was a calligraphic sketch; in charcoal and ink. She noticed me staring foolishly at it.

'Bill did that,' she said.

It hit me in the guts.

'But that's a – Petyt surely. William Petyt!'

'It's Billy all right,' she said with a certain satisfaction.

Petyt had been one of the few whites to 'promote' black sculpture in the country. He is now safely dead and buried in his Canada.

She stroked ash from her cigarette; her fingernails were neither long nor painted. She had become the kind of person who has no need of claws. She said: 'His friend Mike was weird, though. Not utterly. He made me stand naked and astride a sort of bull's-eye thing and he would throw all kinds of jellies right at my hole, you know. And while aiming and all he would chant

67

a thing about the Congo, the Mau Mau, Algeria, and one of our leaders who shall remain nameless.'

I stared.

She shook her head, and stubbed out her cigarette. She yawned.

'Do you want to know about the others?'

I nodded.

'Then ask me another time,' she said, leaning back into her chair and crossing her legs rather loosely. At that moment she looked like the old Nestar for whom I had pined in primary school. I was then so smitten by her that, until one painful day when the teacher compared my handwriting with the handwriting in her book, I did all her homework and was prepared to consign the universe into a flushing toilet.

I turned sharply.

The doorhandle was turning slowly, noiselessly. The door opened. A tall youth who wore his body the way a traveller lugs a heavy trunk walked in. He looked as though nails had been driven into his palms and into his feet. He planted himself directly before me.

'What do you want with my mother, munt? Begging for arse? You fucking stinking nigger ...'

I slid my hand into my coat and casually brought out an evil-looking Okapi. Nestar sat up staring. I did not even look at him. Knives were not that strange to me.

'What was that you said?'

He seemed to lick his lips with a swallowing noise like a flying fish splashing clumsily back into the sea. I could feel him sizing me up; weighing his chances. I decided to haul my fish out of the water. I had recognised him as soon as he came into the room. I looked up at him.

He half-turned towards Nestar.

'Ma ...'

But she shrugged her hands of the whole question. I panned the Okapi point over the area of his belly. I must confess I felt like a tainted, sullied black hero.

'Remember a girl called Anne?' I asked.

He stiffened.

Nestar raked him with her impassive brown eyes.

I said: 'She is my best friend's sister. And she's still in hospital. I don't want to know why you did it.'

Nestar contemplated a spot somewhere behind my right shoulder.

'What happened?' she asked.

'He beat her up and screwed her while she was senseless or something.'

I knew she had instantly come over to my side. But she obviously did not like doing so.

I backed towards the phone. I dialled.

My dialling finger was stained with the ink from the pen I had used to jot down Nestar's story.

'Philip? I've found the bastard. Come over right now and we'll get it over with.'

I gave him the address. I added: 'That means we're quits about Julia, aren't we?'

His reply to that was correctly indistinct.

Ten minutes later Philip bounded into the room. There was no baggage of fat on his person; indeed he looked very fit. As if there was a spark within him which constantly maddened him into a reluctant inertia.

'Him? This kid? This boy? This half and half? This rum and milk character?'

I nodded.

Philip strode right up to him and said: 'I want to hear it from your own lips. Did you do it?'

The boy's eyes rolled the way God, when he had become

69

flesh, could not change himself back into the original Word.

Finally the boy said: 'Yes. But I had taken dagga. I was ...'

But Philip had turned to Nestar.

'Who are you?'

Nestar, shaking out a cigarette from her gold packet, smiled: 'His mother.'

And Philip leaned over her and lit her cigarette.

'How come,' he asked, 'how come you bring your son up wrong?'

Her smile widened until it swallowed the room.

'It's none of your business, is it?' she said.

He swivelled, crouching and kneeling the boy in one smooth action.

The boy doubled up; mouth open like a fish, the hands folded over the pain. A precise blow to the jaw threw the boy clear across the room and he fell crushing on to the Venus statue, which broke into pieces.

Nestar gathered in her legs from the mess.

'Not in here, if you please. The basement is the best place,' she said.

We left her picking up the ruins of Venus.

In the basement Philip said: 'Put that knife away. This is no gangster novel. And this ...!'

The blow smashed into the boy like a pickaxe crushing into a wedding cake.

I slid my knife back into my coat and walked upstairs, leaving Philip to smash the boy into a stain. Stains! Love or even hate or the desire for revenge are just so many stains on a sheet, on a wall, on a page even. This page. Growing up involves this. And Philip was crunching it into him.

Nestar was still picking up the fragments of her divinity. She looked up.

'I could kill you,' she said, smiling.

70

She handed me the statue's crotch.

'You've always wanted that from me,' she said. 'There it is, then.'

I stared at it for a long moment. Was this all there was, then?

Her voice, laughing, brought me back into the room.

'Yes, it's about time you learnt that; isn't it?' she was saying.

'God help us all,' I muttered.

Philip came in. His hands looked like Macbeth's after the murder of Duncan. But when he came closer I saw that those hands were really spotless, clean. He held out his hand to Nestar: 'It's been nice meeting you ...' Philip began.

A stinging slap stopped him, brought the tears into his eyes. She rubbed the deadly palm on her cream gown as though his cheek had dirtied it. She turned to me, with fingers held out for a farewell greeting. I had no sooner taken her hand than I somersaulted through the air and landed heavily at her feet. I was too surprised for words.

'Hey!' Philip exclaimed.

An uppercut threw him brutally against the wall. The impact brought the heavily framed Petyt drawing crashing on to his head.

'Now, get out both of you,' she said helping him to his feet. 'Get out.'

We could not get out fast enough. Ah, heroes, black heroes ...

Sunlight bounced off a grimy phone booth and noiselessly splintered into the glass front of a drowsy coffee shop. I rapped on the counter with a coin – the way Harry does. A white old age pensioner's face slowly rotated into view. It stared hard at us as if we were something shameful like doubtful foreign coins. The pink mouth embedded in meagre strings of pink fat twitched, sticking with saliva like stalagmites and stalactites.

It said: 'Kaffirs at the back. Kaffirs ...'

A globule of saliva oozed gently down on to the khaki safari jacket and broke into tiny diamond rivulets which slithered and settled on to the great paunch of belly. The red eyes regarded us without the slightest interest; a lifeless kind of boredom. A fat black fly retched on a cream bun, washed its hands, and flew with a great laziness on to the sweating pink brow.

Philip leaned over the counter and spat into the aged pink face. But the fat black fly merely continued its business – its own business – in the salt of the old sweat. And the slow red eyes had closed in upon themselves. The mouth, showing an obscene toothless razor wound, spluttered with spittle; mumbled: 'Kaffirs ...'

The oily white-hot sunlight streamed its asphalt-melting energy, casting razor-sharp beams of highlights in the windows. A fat bulldog, tongue stretched out on to the shaded pavement, lazily scanned us with one beady eye. A livid white ring seemed to radiate vividly around the sun. It made me think of the white down on a white dove's breast. Swan-white. And Leda when Zeus transfixed her in mid-air. It made me think of Harry's rubber snake. The white underbelly of a stinking reptile. The stench of it gave the sun a nauseous hue. And it was touching everything. Pushing me into the room and my teeth ached like the chatterclutter of a typewriter. The handcuffs were too tight.

'Another one of them, Sergeant.'

'Communist.'

A little blood trickled down from my wrists.

'Terrorist, huh?'

'Says he's a student at the University.'

'Ach!'

And then up and down into and out of corridors and, I don't know, deep down or high up into a small room. There was only a bench in it. And with the questions and the questions and the questions and the blows, the bench began to grow and grow with my life and my bruises, with my breath and the stains of my blood. Something had gone out of me and into the bench which had come alive with it. Someone was saying, 'Leave me with the fucking cunt for five minutes and he'll talk like never-never.' Something exploded inside my head.

They were looking down at me when I came to. A black plain-clothes policeman was saying something and pointing with his finger down at me. There was a minute crack on his fingernail.

'... just five minutes,' he was saying.

They left me with him.

'I will not bother asking you questions,' he said. 'You know what we want. So, name names. Starting now.'

The bench was a dull ache at the back of my mind.

He took off his coat slowly. He unbuttoned his shirtsleeves and folded them back up to his upper arms. As I watched him come for me, in the instant his fist swung, Julia's face, transfixed by the spikes of a blinding white light, flared inside my mind. Inside the bench. Inside the room. Anaesthetising my soul.

An eternity later, when he could no longer find any spot on my body to hurt and I was still conscious but dead to every blow he could think of, the door opened and the white officers came in. They took one look at me and dragged him off. And the corridor came and stone steps cut into me grazing my knuckles and knees and a foot kicking me tore through the faded cloth of my sanity and they took one hand each and they dragged the endless stone steps into the stains that had once been my raging brains.

The sunlight had imperceptibly grown weaker – there was a brittle tang in the air. The attendant greeted Philip. In the lift I studied my face and with the same old horror stared at my prematurely grey hair. Philip's office was as usual up to its neck with newspapers and magazines. He threw himself into the leather chair behind the desk. I leaned back in the soft visitors' chair. He picked up the phone and told the receptionist that he was now in. I was studying the titles of the books on his desk: Aimé Césaire, LeRoi Jones, James Baldwin, Senghor, and a well-thumbed copy of Christopher Okigbo's poems. He shoved a light blue folder towards me. I began to leaf through it.

There were fifteen poems in all; his own. They expressed forms of discontent, disillusionment and outrage. Clarity, it seemed, had been sacrificed for ugly mood. Even the praises of 'Blackness' had a sour note in them. One felt live coals hissing in a sea of paranoia. Gloomy nights stitched by needles of existentialism. Black despair lit up by suicidal vision. The false dawn, charcoal black, trembling in the after-echoes of passion. And songs of a golden age of black heroes; of myths and legends and sprites. And ghouls. These were the exposed veins dripping through the body of the poems. One of them was about Julia and myself; it was entitled 'Something Rotten'. It reminded me of the time when I was writing an article about shantytown and while inspecting the pit-latrines there I fell into the filthy hole. I am still not quite recovered from the experience. It was in a way a necessary baptism.

'"Baptism" is the title of them all,' Philip said.

'A sort of E R Brathwaite rites of passage?'

'Uhuh.'

He looked at me as though I had said something indecent. He said: 'There is nothing to make one particularly glad one is a human being and not a horse, or a lion, or a jackal, or come to think of it a snake. Snakes. There's just dirt and shit and urine and blood and smashed brains. There's dust and fleas and bloody whites and roaches and dogs trained to bite black people in the arse. There's venereal disease and beer and lunacy and just causes.

74

There's technology to drop on your head wherever you stop to take a leak. There's white shit in our leaders and white shit in our dreams and white shit in our history and white shit on our hands in anything we build or pray for. Even if that was okay there's still sell-outs and informers and stuck-up students and get-rich-fast bastards and live-now-think-later punks who are just as bad, man. Just as bad as white shit. There's a lot of these bastards hanging around in London waiting to come back here and become cabinet ministers. The only cabinet they'll be in is a coffin. Don't get me wrong. I'm a pessimist, but I still add two and two and walk to the seven, smiling. You find friends and things happen to them, and the thunderstorm in their minds is staring incredibly out of their eyes. You mind your own business and the business springs up and hits you right between the eyes. You bang your head on the wall and the wall crumbles and there's another wall and you wake up with the whole Earth one big headache inside your head. You tuck your tail between your legs and some enterprising vandal sets fire to your fur, as you streak through the dry grass of your fears. And when you stop by that wall to figure out the next poem some character empties a heavy chamberpot of slogans right on top of your head. There's a lot of anger gets you nowhere. There's heaps of consideration gets you nowhere too. It's just tickets to nowhere, everything is. There's big men now. There'll be big men always to dig pit-latrines for you and your children to fall in. I don't give no heat to any lecherous system. I just fuck and screw myself in a quiet green place and load my balls on to my shoulders for the big trip beyond the grave. There's hungry people out there. There's homeless people out there. There's many going about in the rags of their birthday suit. And they's all mad. They's all got designs. You've got designs. I've got designs. But we're all designing in a sea full of shit. There's clouds of flies everywhere you go, flies eating our dead. There's armies of worms slithering in our history. And there's squadrons of mosquitoes homing

75

down on to the cradle of our future. What do we do? Clutch and drown each other, that's what, and if we can't do ourselves in properly there's congregations of missionaries and shrinks to do it and they have on their side cops and soldiers and Australia and New Zealand and Britain and China and the USA and France and the bloody Germans. The poor are not the only ones who've got designs!'

He took a deep breath. And sinking back into his chair he placed an ankle over a knee and began to light a cheap cigar. I almost asked him where the rolled cigarette was. I couldn't even laugh; it was too chilling.

'Nothing lasts long enough to make any sense,' I said.

I said it without conviction.

I went on: 'There are fragments and snatches of fragments. The momentary fingerings of a guitar. Things as they are – but not really in the Wallace Stevens manner. The way things have always been. A torn bit of newspaper whose words have neither beginning nor end but the words upon it. A splinter of melody piercing the ear with a brittle note. Nothing lasts long enough to have been. These fragments of everything descend upon us haphazardly. Only rarely do we see the imminence of wholes. And that is the beginning of art.'

He had been holding his breath; now he breathed out, seeming to contract into the leather of his chair. He regarded me with the eye of a fly that, floating in a bowl of soup, looks up straight into the diner's soul. Finally he threw a newspaper into my lap. He had marked out with red ink an article about a battle between Smith's security forces and the guerrillas; two large pictures accompanied it. The photographs showed twenty-two dead guerrillas laid out for display and in the centre of them stood the 'prisoner', a dead-looking youth staring morosely at the camera. He had, it said, been captured during the fierce engagement. There was something about him which I felt I

76

ought to –

'Remember him?' Philip asked quietly.

It hit me like a spring in the box. I remembered that brutally scarred face. The captured guerrilla was Edmund. At school he had been small, undernourished, and extremely poor. Everyone, including myself, had always been nasty to him because he refused to have anything to do with our student armchair politics. He had been utterly lonely; everyone was simply rude to him. But he would lock himself in the boxroom and study all night every week. In class he sat in the corner at the back writing voluminous notes which in reality were mere transcripts of almost every book in the library. But every term he would be at the bottom of the class. He did not take part in any games. His father, a primary school teacher, had died of alcoholic poisoning after a fantastic night out on the town with my father. His mother, a nurse, had been unable to cope and suddenly took to her bed and repulsed violently all attempts to coax her from it. But destitution knocked on her door and so frightened her that she, one morning, put on her best dress, straightened her hair, painted her face and made a bee-line to the nearest beer hall where her figure aroused some interest. It was she who had coached Nestar.

I stared hard at the photographs; the corpses looked as if they had been dead for quite a while. One face seemed to be nothing but a mass of flies. And Edmund stood morosely erect among them. Sole survivor. At school he had stood among us in such a manner and had, it seemed, doggedly lived out his tortured dreams in the face of humiliation. I do not know why he liked me – but he did. He could not read enough of Gogol; he even tried to teach himself Russian so that he could read him in the original. He was the only one in the class who knew that Yevtushenko really existed. Dostoyevsky, Chekhov, Turgenev, Pushkin, Gorky – he read them all. But he thought Gogol the best of them. And he would set off the tiny firecrackers of his laughter as he read

The Government Inspector. He regarded Shostakovitch as the best of composers; and thought Moussorgsky 'good'. Among painters, Edmund had long singled out Hieronymus Bosch as his master. When I asked him what he would do when school and university were over he said that he wanted to write. He had actually written dozens of novels (all unfinished) and short stories (all unfinished) whose plots alternated between the painstaking exploration of the effects of poverty and destitution on the 'psyche' and the higher themes of grand dramas and heroic epics that would be concerned with something of what Gogol tried to do for the Russian character. In our first year his bed was next to mine in Dormitory Four. His locker was lavishly decorated with reproductions of portraits of the Devil and with enlarged texts of Satan's speeches culled from Milton's *Paradise Lost*.

The first night in the dormitory Edmund entertained us with a species of farting which by midnight made it necessary to ventilate the room by opening all the windows even though the night was extremely chilly. The noise of it disturbed Jet, the assistant boarding master who we knew was entertaining the cook's wife in the flat attached to our dormitory.

Jet strutted into our dormitory just as our prefect was about to lecture Edmund on the uses and abuses of breaking wind. His torch flashed into my near-sighted eyes and then veered on to Edmund's face.

'You again!' Jet remonstrated.

He had caught Edmund spitting about in the dining room, that afternoon.

'Where do you come from?'

Jet was using his special voice, one specifically cultivated for talking to idiots.

Edmund told him.

'Did they teach you there to gas people to death?'

'No.'

78

'What is your totem?'

'Nguruwe.'

'Very appropriate,' Jet agreed with sarcasm.

Jet was a well-built coal-black character of average height whose favourite gesture was cracking his finger joints in the most striking manner, especially when the schoolgirls were anywhere within twenty miles of his person. He invariably dressed in flower-printed shirts, with a handkerchief neatly strangling his neck, and purple trousers. Purple was his colour – not anyone else's; and all newcomers learnt this quickly and kissed their purple things, especially underwear, goodbye.

Now he danced slowly to and fro and cracked his fingers absently.

'Most appropriate indeed,' he repeated.

He was later to be sacked for 'carrying on' with one of the African nuns who were attached to the mission.

'You will report to me at nine o'clock tomorrow morning,' he said.

He was clipping the words like a gardener snipping the last touches to the hedge of Life.

The prefect at last intervened: 'The boy deserves another chance, sir. After all, the first day is always rather ...'

He never finished his sentence because at that moment Edmund who could no longer contain his gut leaned over to one side and let out right in my face a painfully devastating fart. I'm now quite recovered.

'Who would have thought it of Edmund?' Philip coughed and racked phlegm down his throat.

'I would; don't you remember his fight with Stephen?'

Philip nodded ambiguously.

The telephone shrilled. As he spoke into the long black shape, I let my eyes rove once more around the office. This was what mother had always wanted me to become. My eyes lit on *To the Point*, a stupid Boer magazine on African current affairs.

The Edmund–Stephen fight was the most talked-about event the year it happened. It even outclassed Smith's UDI. This is how it happened. Stephen was older, bigger and broader than anyone else in the first form. Stephen was mean, a bully; a typical African bully in an ordinary African school. He had appropriated for his own specific use such notable figures as Nkrumah, Kaunda, Che, Castro, Stalin, Mao, Kennedy, Nyerere and, for that matter, everyone else who could be dragged into an after-hours dormitory argument. Stephen genuinely loathed Edmund; it was like a rat and a cat, or a cat and a dog, or a dog and a crocodile or a crocodile and the Tarzan we saw twice a term in the Great Hall. Stephen detested 'classical' music. And for some reason Stephen thought that Gogol was the one great enemy of Africa who had to be stamped out at all cost. Stephen was an avid reader of the Heinemann African Writers Series. He firmly believed that there was something peculiarly African in anything written by an African and said that therefore European tools of criticism should not be used in the analysis of 'African literature'. He had also gleaned a few nuggets of thought from E. Mphahlele's *The African Image*. And he had a lifestyle to go with it: he was nearly expelled for refusing to go to mass and to prayers – he said 'Christianity is nothing but a lie; seek ye the political kingdom and everything else will follow'; he was always taking the geography master to task about his ironic comments about the primitive state of Africa's roads; he was always petitioning for African history to be taught – the only history we were taught was British and European, with the United States for dessert. He took dagga; he believed that there is a part of man which is permanently stoned and that this was beautiful. He said that there is a part of man which never ages and that this part of the human make-up does not move with things but moves them, transcends them and best manifests itself only when the things that move are on the brink of stillness. Stephen also had nightmares, great gouts of them; and he was ashamed of this one 'weakness'. His fearful screams could be heard almost every night; and he would try not to sleep by provoking endless discussion on almost everything under the sun. One day he let it be known that Edmund's mother was a 'common drunken whore' and that he, Stephen, had screwed her nuts and she had certainly used some of the money to pay for Edmund's fees. I knew there was some truth in Stephen's unexpected announcement. The dormitory was stunned, not so much by the news as by the weight of ill-feeling behind it. Even Stephen seemed to be aware that he had irrevocably broken things that should never be broken: except at a heavy price.

Edmund, in a surprisingly calm voice, broke the silence.

He challenged Stephen to a fight.

The dormitory laughed. I laughed, too.

Stephen laughed.

I tugged at Edmund's pyjama-sleeve, warningly.

But he brushed me aside and said out loud: 'Then you must take back everything you said and apologise to me before the whole dormitory.'

The dormitory tittered. Uneasily.

Stephen, now aware that his design was about to be fulfilled, said: 'You've all heard what the Pig has said. He is farting in our faces again. I've never refused a challenge; Africa always rises up to every new challenge, as Nkrumah said. Even the challenge of immorality, and snivelling tsotsis like this semen-drop of a bastard.'

He calmly walked up to Edmund and hit him, contemptuously with the back of his hand; Edmund's head snapped back, knocking against the locker.

I gripped Edmund's arm.

'For God's sake, this is not a Petersburg story. He's for real.

A brute. He'll simply thrash you.'

But Edmund had set his face towards Jerusalem; his eyes were red, smarting from the sting of Stephen's blow. A strange fatalism seemed to have suddenly aged him.

'What else is there?' he asked me quietly.

Even the prefect tried to intervene – I think he liked Edmund the way a village is jealous of its local eccentric.

But Edmund only said: 'What else is there?'

The fight took place the next day, a Saturday, in the clearing where the Boy Scouts and the Girl Guides usually paraded.

I did not go to watch.

It seemed hours before everyone returned; everyone, that is, except Edmund. Their silence alarmed me. But a small hairy boy whom I was later to know as Philip rushed up to me and said hoarsely: 'He won't let anyone help him; but I know he'll listen to you. You're friends, aren't you? He's just lying there in his blood. What remains of him. He's stark staring mad. Not raving, no. Just wallowing in his own blood ...'

Stephen came out of the bathroom, wiping his hands and staring ruefully at his bruised knuckles. There was blood on his shirt; a rather large stain which seemed in outline to be a map of Rhodesia. Where was Edmund? Philip saw him too and stopped talking. I ran blindly to the scout clearing where they had left him.

He was on his hands and knees in a pool of blood. His face was unrecognisable. And he was whining; jabbering distractedly like an animal. I almost cried when I finally understood what it was he was saying; he was saying over and over 'I'm a monkey, I'm a baboon, I'm a monkey, I'm a baboon.' Most of his front teeth had gone and his jaw seemed to be hanging on by a thread. Great scabs of blood were forming all over his eyes, nose, mouth, and cheeks. I picked him up in my arms and carried him straight to the clinic. He was not heavy. And his thin broken voice saying over and over 'I'm a monkey, I'm a baboon, I'm a baboon,' this too was not heavy. I understood it only too well.

Sister Catherine took one look at him and said: 'He'll have to go to the hospital.' And she picked up the phone to call the principal's office.

When the school lorry drove off taking Edmund to the hospital in Umtali the principal asked me who had done it.

I shook my head.

'He'll tell you himself when he is well,' I said. 'If he wants to,' I added.

I was tired. My mind was numb. I began to pick at my lips.

They wired his jaw. They used a lot of stitches to save something of that crushed-in face. Yards of stitches. The term was almost over when he came back to the school. He said nothing; not a word about Stephen. His scarred face had become more pronounced in its moroseness; its particular features seemed to have been stitched together by a fatalistic self-disgust. Smith announced his unilateral declaration of independence. I wrote a short story based on the fight but, as soon as I finished it, tore it up in disgust when I saw Edmund's stitched-together warthog face. There, in the photograph.

I returned the newspaper to Philip.

He lit a cigarette.

'You can cut the picture out if you like,' he said.

Why not? I wondered.

I picked up the tiny scissors.

Doug and Citre came in. Faded jeans. Denim shirts. Citre had studied English Literature at Durban and was now worried about being drafted into the army. Doug had, after art school in London, tried making films and had ended up in the advertising racket. Doug was a windbreaker, very earnest, with a long angular face and low but wide shoulders that had around them the unwashed elegance of uncompromising youth. Citre, taller, leaner, had the unease of a shambling giraffe that is learning to walk, all legs and neck; seriously doubtful; and given to putting his points sheepishly – altogether a likeable, clumsy youth.

Doug drove us all to Citre's house. While we waited for the other guests to arrive we shared pipes of dagga and sampled Doug's marijuana biscuits. Citre as usual stammered something political by way of putting Philip and I at our ease.

'Politics is shit,' Doug said thoughtfully.

I agreed.

'White people are shit,' Doug added with closed eyes.

I agreed.

'And black people are shit,' Doug blew cinders and ash from his shirtfront.

Before I could agree again Philip interrupted: 'Everybody human shits, that's the trouble.'

I nodded, watching my mind explode deliciously.

There was this mirror and I was watching my head nodding in slow motion. It seemed I could go on nodding and agreeing forever. It was so sweet I could not bear it.

'Do you like the music?' Citre asked.

I had to make an effort to stop myself looking clean through the clear crystals of his words.

'What music?' I asked.

I was a big bird high up in God's own spaces where the music of the spheres is so still that all man's ordinary delight becomes nothing. I was a lone eagle, hovering, swivelling tautly on the golden axis of a heady sunset. In one of Solomon's photographs. Christ!

'You're nodding to it,' Citre said and raised the volume a little.

I said, 'Oh!'

Then Doug turned off the lights and switched on a cine

projector on to a white canvas hanging down on the far wall. The first film was of an old black man, rags tucked in, cycling into town. Thin stringy hands gripping ice-cold handlebars. Bare feet pedalling mechanically on and on and on. And tired owl eyes that stared straight into the spying lens. The second film was a ruthless close-up shot – five minutes long – of a black woman nestling and hushing a white baby to sleep. The baby's satiated pink moonface puffed in and out slowly and its small blue eyes sleepily contemplated a single long hair on the black woman's chin. The third film was of five people, three men and two women in a lift forever going upwards – or had the lift stopped, or was it going downwards? – and all self-consciously staring at the numbers which were flickering randomly on and off. The fourth film was made from newspaper cuttings. It began with the camera lens exactly scanning a ten-minute list of Births and Marriages and then shifted abruptly to focus on the black and white pictures. Of the pictures shown there were many of traffic snarl-ups and ghastly road accidents (one of the victims was the old man cycling in the first film). Close-ups of violent rugby scenes. A firing squad shooting the woman who led the 1896–7 uprising – she looked like the woman in the second film. Excerpts from industrial accidents; and then a fifteen minute long section of the unending Deaths and Funerals classified ads. Doug shot on to this strips of public figures making private speeches. Finally a baby painstakingly spelling with its bricks THE END. The fifth was the one I had been waiting for. Doug had shot Patricia and I in the throes of rather violent intercourse. I had not seen the film because of a little trouble with the police. The sixth was of Julia being screwed by Citre. I had seen it before but had not appreciated its finer points. Doug interposed upon it a strip of Ian Smith declaring UDI. And the last film was of a ballpoint drawing a series of question marks.

'And that, gentlemen, is my novel,' Doug laughed as he

switched on the lights. I looked around at the others who had arrived during the films. They were casually scattered about the room in a landscape of blood-red gaudy poufs and cushions. In the far corner Patricia was peering near-sightedly at the jacket of Vivaldi's *Four Seasons*. John, a mathematician who had lent me his old battered typewriter the day before, was delivering an unconvincing argument for elitist government. His audience was a pimply youth who played drums for a local jazz band. And languidly lounging on the wine-dark bed were three girls, triplets, quite identical, who were sipping Bristol Cream; they were all studying anthropology but seemed not to have been amused after sampling Malinovski, Radcliffe-Brown and Evans-Pritchard. Their tiny pink mouths seemed to 'be perpetually contracting into some inward amusement.

And seated Buddha-like in the centre of the room was Richter, a student of something mystic and obscure whose word-drawings had become fashionable just then. I had met Richter by chance. He was, like me, a solitary drinker. In the Union he always sat apart at the far end of the veranda drinking strong and strange mixtures of pure spirit. Then the military got hold of him and, when the whole length of it was through with him, there was almost nothing left but locust-like raspings of wings in his mind. He had become one of those characters upon whom silence rather than intellect bestows a certain transcendental dignity. At times, however, he meticulously dissected that silence for us, scalpelling it to its very entrails and with a sterile pin pointing out to us organs of interest. These were invariably harrowing accounts of atrocities he had either witnessed or taken part in, in the operational area.

Richter died recently. He was crunched to a stain by a train as he wandered about in the early hours through the town in a drugged and drunken stupor. But there he was, now. Cold, white, as though already dead; wrapped up in a membrane of silence, and sitting still as though studying the abyss into which he must fall.

Richter would not be Richter without the staining of those baptismal scars, I thought, watching him.

At this point Athena strolled in quite casually in the shape of Ada, Nestar's daughter. Like Nestar, she has the resilience and cutting edge of a diamond. She dressed in nothing but light shades of brown and chocolate. A long necklace of polished agates drooped over her uplifted breasts. She sank into a cushion beside Philip.

She smiled quite disarmingly.

'I hear you've been doing things to my brother,' she said, revealing a gold tooth.

Concerned, Philip looked pained.

'How is he?' he asked.

But she smiled the room into her mind: 'How is your sister?' she asked.

'Mending well.'

'And so is he,' she said, freezing up.

The glint of her large silver-plated earrings pulsed like a distant star sending out signals to the last man on Earth. We were so many light-years from each other it frightened me a little. But the fact of contact itself held out hope – if not an open door. There would be gatherings such as these; of memories and of the dead who have never been gone. And those to come who have always been here. But it is as if it was God's wound and we were the maggots slithering in it. And, satiated with the great purposelessness of it, we gently belched nerve gases into the next generation. Ada was one of those who walk the tightrope smiling a scathing scorn at the blind reverses of chance; neither looking up nor looking down – just walking calmly into the crocodile's jaws. Richter passed the peace-pipe to her. The twittering triplets were unconcernedly listening to Robert's fragmentary account of his band's tour of South Africa. Patricia fingered a silver flute and blew an indistinctly sweet note; and then, frowning, she peered into the mouthpiece and after shaking it began to play to herself. I sat down on a cushion facing her.

She had dropped out of the university and without a word disappeared from view. She had done this after she and I had been beaten up by some right-wing demonstrators. Her parents then hired a private detective to search for her. He found her six months later living in a shantytown outside Cape Town. She exhibited her paintings and batiks and got good reviews. But she disappeared again soon after the exhibition. They found her in a sort of opium den in the Chinese quarter. She made a terrible scene and things could not be kept out of the newspapers. But the air soon cleared and she was left to her own devices. She painted furiously. When she put on another exhibition the police confiscated several of her drawings and paintings and there was talk of a subversion-of-morals charge. She could not stand it: she tore down the rest, slashed them to pieces and danced on them like someone dancing on a loved one's grave. It was now difficult to disappear anywhere in Southern Africa. Malawi, perhaps. Ada gave her the name of a Greek person who quickly obliged after the payment of an undisclosed sum. She disappeared for the third time. Those who knew said she was roaming through Africa with nothing but a cheap camera and pencils and sketchbooks. I worried and Harry sharpened his sarcasm at my expense.

She returned half-blind, feverish, and with her voice gone. She was in hospital for weeks and they would not let me see her because it was a Whites Only hospital. They managed to save her sight. But she would never be able to talk again.

She passed the peace-pipe to me and began to riffle through her canvas bag. She took out a book and handed it to me. There was a tiny burning in her eyes; a fierce tenderness I had never seen before. No, I had seen it before – in Immaculate. I leafed through the book.

It slowly paralysed my face.

I hugged her awkwardly like a pessimist who will not believe either his senses or his mind: they had published her notebooks that very day! She reached out for my face and kissed me till I was breathless and full of belief.

Patricia is five feet two. Green eyes. Light sandy hair piled loosely back down to her waist. Though certainly plain, as Harry had said, meaning to wound me, and, when feeling lazy, rather dowdy, Patricia is one of those disturbingly concise and adult youths whom our country either breaks or confines in prisons and lunatic asylums. We were watching the right-wing demonstration (demanding the racial segregation of the halls of residence) when she just said: 'I've got to get out of this!'

I was lying flat on my belly watching the defiant placards (Blacks Out! Whites In!! Segregation Is Honest Integration!!!) and she was kneeling and her lips seemed to have worried themselves to a decision.

She wrung my hand: 'Let's both get out of this.'

But I – the fool! – shook my head sadly and told her parrot-fashion all the good reasons for my not 'getting out of this'.

But she persisted: 'It's easy,' she said. 'We'll just walk off campus and never come back and just keep trying to get out of this wretched country. We'll run to Botswana. And from Gaborone fly to London. I'll paint and you'll write. There'll be ...'

One of the demonstrators had come up; and was staring with venom at her. He began to curse: 'You bitch. Kaffir-lover. Kafferboetie. You cunt. You ...'

I got up slowly.

He swung: 'And you – !'

I ducked beneath the wild blow, grabbed his head from behind and, straightening abruptly, butted him making his jaws crack. Behind him the other demonstrators were massing up, looking ugly. I hurled her up on to her feet: 'Run!'

Punched another down and followed her.

They were after us in an instant. We did not stand a chance, she and I; no one would intervene to try to help us because she and I had dared to flaunt our horns and hooves to our respective racial groups. She could not run much because of her club-foot. I could hear her gasping with pain. The sky spun around her crazily.

Out of the corner of my eye I saw running shapes converging madly towards us. I almost blundered into her body as she fell. There were white faces all around us. Full of blood. The pink flesh peeled back over the teeth. Those claws! In that moment – the half-second before the blows began to fly – I studied each particular white face intimately; noting a pimple here, a hairlip there, shining eyes, furry nostrils, dark circles around blue eyes, a tousled face, a hamslab of a face, a skeletal face –

The impact of my fist on the hairlip jolted through my knuckles to my gut. Patricia was trying to get up, scratching a face, bashing the pimple with her little fists. The person of the skeletal face had thrown his foot to kick her in the stomach when I turned lashing out at his flying foot with my own: as he somersaulted into the air I crouched beneath him and heaved. He crashed into five of his friends. A massive rock of a fist – it was the character with the hamslab of a face – crushed half my face and I began to bleed. Becoming a stain. Stains! I punched and at the same time kicked him hard on the shin and as he leaned forward I snapped his head back with my left. Patricia was again down there in the mass of kicking feet.

Maddened by desperation, I began to fight like a lunatic around her. I punched, jabbed, hooked, smote the bloody Philistines. I smashed, swiped and drove into them. She was screaming painfully, being trampled. I pelted them with the hail-stones of desperation. I stoned them with the rocks of fear. I tore into them. They were tiring me out. I scratched, mauled, flailed, and threshed into those too many white faces. But they hammered into me until I had lost so much blood that I wondered if I was still alive. They slammed into me, banged me where it hurt, and kept knocking me from every direction. I did not – must not – dare fall and cover my face with my hands; they would simply plough into me. I smacked them right back, buffeted them down, thumped them back, whacked them down, as they pummelled and pounded and battered into me. I kicked, booted, kneed, and cudgelled into them as they bulldozed into me and pile-drove me into one lump of pain. I clubbed, coshed, slugged, whipped, flogged and bashed into them as they sledge-hammered into me. She was down there, not moving, her shirt ripped to reveal a dirty bra. I slammed out with an uppercut and the last thing I saw was a cold white face paralysed by a massive rush of blood. And then I crashed out across her body ...

Those stitches. Those stitches, each one exactly biting after the needle's penetration; each one a little stained with blood; they have nipped me maddeningly.

My earliest memory is of the skies swinging askew, and I falling out of an apple tree. The fall merely bruised my hands and knees. Mother washed them with hot salted water and I remember her cunning face peering down anxiously into the cot where I lay contemplating my first encounter with the real world. And then I had eye trouble; my eyes stinging painfully through clear globules of spinning sunlight. And my first fever which neither aspirins or Cafenol could abate; this was when I learned to be wary of my own imagination and of my mind. I still do not quite know whether the flood was rising or it was my body that was gradually falling into that great fright of waters. Afterwards the door had to be securely locked and barred against my sleep-walking. The nganga was called. He made half-inch incisions all over my body and rubbed a black powder into the tiny wounds.

A pot of something like porridge was cooked and as it boiled furiously he made me lean over it breathing in the steam and he threw a blanket over me as I did so.

The other thing I remember clearly from my childhood is a huge dog staring at me from the enclosed back seat of a car. My parents had taken me to visit someone in the African hospital and I had somehow wandered into the car park; and stopped to gape at the shaggy beast in one of the cars. Its eyes were black and clear. It was a clearness without any depth to it and this made me automatically trust it. Its nose was soft and black, its ears neatly wadded down to cover massive jaws. I felt that beast in me keenly. And as it pressed against the window and let its great eyes pierce into me I irresistibly put out my hand to open the door for it to be free. The instant the door noiselessly clicked the beast, growling, rushed its massive weight against the door and was upon me with its bared fangs.

There are flies squashed to the memory. Congregations spinning out webs of prayers to catch the minute nuggets of revelation. Inkstains, watercolours, chalk, pastel drawings, tearstains, bloodstains, time charts, posters of the life cycle of fleas and once more inkstains ... Dirty fingers scratching into obscure orifices; blurred images sneaking deeper into the flea-crevices of the mind. And what once was our parents now rotted and stank beneath the lime of the twentieth century. An iron net had been thrown over the skies, quietly. Now it, tightening, bit sharply into the tenderer meat of our brains. The hard knocks it gave to our heads made us strange, even to ourselves. And beneath it all our minds festered; gangrenous. Gangsterish. The underwear of our souls was full of holes and the crotch it hid was infested with lice. We were whores; eaten to the core by the syphilis of the white man's coming. Masturbating on to a *Playboy* centrefold; screaming abuse at a solitary but defiant racist; baring our arse to the yawning pit-latrine; writing angry 'black' poetry;

screwing pussy as though out to prove that White men do not in reality exist – this was all contained within the circumvention of our gut-rot.

Those stitches like a net cast up into the sky tightened around the mind, and with the needle bit sharply into the tenderer parts of the brain.

I saw Philip safely home; he was in worse shape than I was. We had said our farewells to Doug and Citre and Richter and Patricia and Ada and the twittering chorus of triplets. I staggered home.

Two shadows detached themselves from the dark. I did not know them. They stood blocking my way.

'We've been looking for you,' the shorter one said.

They had drawn nearer.

'You beat up our friend bad, man. You beat up Leslie, man. Nobody beats up Leslie, didn't you know that?' he said.

Leslie was Nestar's son.

I took a step backwards. My palms were sweating.

The tall one spat: 'Fuck shit!' and caught me solidly on the jaw. I heard my dentures crack beneath the impact. I turned to run but the shorter one stuck out his foot and I fell heavily on to the paved path. They were kicking at my head. I was trying to spit out the fragments of my dentures. I realised I was screaming for help. I tore away. I was thinking: there goes my shoe! Only the tall one came after me, kicking out wide to trip me. He was too close for me to dart into one of the doorways and rouse somebody in the houses sweeping by. I fell too quickly for him and he toppled over me. I was up and into a doorway in an instant, my hands about to bang on the door when he grabbed me and yanked me hard against the low brick garden wall and began to smash my head into it. I screamed louder, hoping someone in the house would hear. With an effort I broke away, kicked out with the shoeless foot and desperately jumped at a window, hollering.

I smashed a fist through the window, cutting my wrist badly and howled for help through the great hole. His hand clamped over my mouth and he dragged me from the window and through the open gate into the paved pathway where he thrashed me so much I blacked out, speechless.

I came to slowly. I was alone on that stretch of road. And rather surprised that I was still alive. I had not known that the body could bear so much pain. I dragged myself up, limped through the gate, and began knocking on the door again. There was not a sound, not a light within; not a single sign to say there was anything human living there.

I turned the door handle. The door immediately opened. I walked in. There were no curtains on the windows; and the wind and light streaming through the broken one showed me that this was a big black empty room. There was nothing in it; no furniture, nothing; nothing at all. My mind felt like nothing. My face certainly felt broken in. A doorway yawned blankly into me: it led to a smaller room: numb, dark and also utterly empty. I could not bring myself to touch the walls to prove that they were really there. After all, the window certainly had been there and had smashed quite conclusively. For some reason I began to wonder if *I* was really in there; perhaps I was a mere creation of the rooms themselves. Another doorway brooded just ahead of me. It led on to a tiny veranda that looked out over an overgrown wilderness of garden into the starry dark-blue immensity of the night. Was there then nothing here also? Had I called out for nothing? I took a step down from the veranda and as I did so something big and sly slouched suddenly through that wilderness of weeds and maize stalks and disappeared through a hole in the far garden wall. My hand involuntarily rose to my head: the sudden pain had been as though a sliver of the grey matter of my brains had been plucked cleanly with a pair of tweezers.

I ran from that house like a madman who has seen the inside

of his own ravings. Somehow I got to a phone and surprised an ambulance which actually turned up and drove me to the African hospital. The doctor sewed up my wrist and took X-rays of my head. And a tetanus injection. But he let me see the X-rays on an illuminated screen. The sight of my bones chilled me. I laughed uneasily. There was nothing to my mind, to my head, but a skull that had some of its grinning teeth missing. That broken grin, I have never been 'able to erase it out of my mind. And the picture of my skull has since blended into the memory of that empty but strangely terrifying house which – when I called – merely maintained an indistinct silence.

It was the House of Hunger that first made me discontented with things. I knew my father only as the character who occasionally screwed mother and who paid the rent, beat me up, and was cuckolded on the sly by various persons. He drove huge cargo lorries, transporting groundnut oil to Zambia and Zaire and Malawi. I knew that he was despised, because of mother, and because he always wore khaki overalls, even on Sundays, and because he was quite generous with money to friends and enemies alike. The only thing was that he was an alcoholic.

He once got Peter and I so drunk that mother thrashed the three of us and then shoved him out of the house for the night. The only time he came close to hitting mother was when she discovered in his travelling bag a quite elaborate set of anti-VD paraphernalia: injections, pills, penicillin, which she threw out into the dustbin. One night the ambulance came and he was in it and they wanted someone to go with him. 'What's wrong with him?' she asked. 'He's been stabbed.' And she got in and it drove off leaving me and Peter to fend for ourselves. I found out later that he had been stabbed by the up to then harmless township idiot. Father was never himself after that: he turned to meths. And some nights he would have the trembling fits and not know what he was doing or what he was saying, while his hands shook and twitched uncontrollably. He would not know where he was, or who he was, or who we were, or where the toilet was. And he would talk about the 'flies'. Apparently when he was in that state he would be tormented by the Furies, who would come to him in the form of a dense cloud of houseflies all humming and singing Handel's 'Hallelujah Chorus'.

But mother was more feared than respected. She was a hard worker in screwing, running a home, and maintaining a seemingly tight rein over her husband; she was good in fights, and verbal sallies, never losing face; and, more important for me, she had nothing better to do than to throw her children into the lion's den of things white. Peter took after her, while I was more my father. Certainly father could never control Peter – only mother could do that; and therefore father handled me severely.

Peter, of course, early became the enemy of all fathers and mothers who had daughters. He and mother gave to the House a whiff of scandal strong enough to be detected throughout the whole region. When Peter became twenty-one father gave him, for a present, a new anti-VD set. Mother merely warned Peter not to get involved with married women. And I – rather grudgingly, for I was extremely jealous – gave him my dubious blessing.

I was by then more experienced in books and masturbation than in girls and street-fights and throwing dice. Whenever mother took away my sheets to wash them she would make me explain every single stain on them. Since they were invariably stained with semen she would contemptuously give me a long sermon about how girls are 'easy' and 'why don't you get on with laying one or two?' Or three. Or four. Or five. 'There is nothing to it,' she said. 'You stick it in the hole between the water and the earth, it's easy. She splays out her legs and you bunch your pelvis between her thighs and Strike! right there between her water and her earth. You strike like a fire and she'll take you and your balls all in. Right? Up to your neck. When you come you'll see it misting her eyes. Don't stop; go on digging. Digging. And she'll heave you in up to the hairs on your head. See? Now. Why don't you get on with laying one and stop messing my sheets? You were late in getting off my breast; you were late in getting out of bedwetting. Now you're late jerking off into some bitch. You make me sick up to here, do you understand? Up to here. It must be those stupid books you're reading – what do you want to read books for when you've finished with the university? Yes, up to here.'

But the old man was my friend. He simply wandered into the House one day out of the rain, dragging himself on his knobby walking stick. And he stayed. His face was like a mesh of copper wire; his wrists, strings of muscle; and his broken body looked so brittle and insubstantial that a strong wind or an expletive would probably have blown him right back into the rain. His broken teeth, tobacco-stained, were those of an ancient horse which even the boiler of glue would reject. But his deep-set eyes, the colour of fire reflected in water, were as full of stories as his tongue was quick to tell them. He would sun himself in the happy company of the local chorus of flies and choke on some secret chuckle. He would take out his tobacco pouch and slowly roll a cigarette, using strips of the *Herald*. What he loved best was for me to listen attentively while he told stories that were oblique, rambling, and fragmentary. His transparent, cunning look, his eager chuckle, his wheezing cough, and something of the earth, gravel-like, in his voice – these gave body to the fragments of things which he casually threw in my direction.

He would begin suddenly: 'A hunter of women. Now to hunt something in yourself is foolish. Because. He screamed in his sleep on the fire of the hunt. When he finally woke up he was up there in the eye of the sky. Fiercely on fire. The sun.

'... cast out of village, town and country. Cast out of womb, home, family. A veritable desert. Of all the grains of despair. He fed on his discontent; but it did not fill up his belly. He fed on his hatred of all things; but that did not quench his thirst. And then he fed on dreams, all kinds, of vengeance, of forgiveness, of self-mutilation, of the love that is in all things. But even that did not quench his thirst, neither did it fill his hunger. For it was a strange thirst. An unknown hunger. Which had driven him from himself, from his friends, from his family, from the things of his first world. He wandered alone and bareheaded under the sun. He fed on exhaustion of mind and body, but the brain only dies at its own behest and the body is a precious thing which, fading and knotting within itself, generates a new being who shimmers around the old body and does not die unless the great star comes down. And so exhaustion did not slake his thirst and weariness, did not stop the gnawing of hunger in his belly. He came to a great city, but when he tried to enter, the guard at the gates laughed a great laugh and the whole thing faded into nothing but sand-dunes. It may not even have been there. There were great beautiful birds in his vision, but when he called out to them they turned into vultures and squawked awkwardly out of his sight. It was like a sudden irritation. In fact he actually scratched himself tenderly between his legs. That's when he said: "I will live at the heart of a grain of sand." And he also said: "I will light a match: when it flares I will jump straight into the dark heart of its flame-seed." But as he listened to himself, to the thirst and to the hunger, he suddenly said in words of gold: "I will live at the head of the stream where all of man's questions begin."'

The old man took out his pouch and in silence rolled a cigarette. His face – that tight mesh of copper wire – stretched a little; smiling in every stitch.

He said: 'There was a race of men in Africa whose women were bottles. And in every bottle there was a ship. Now the men valued the ships highly, but did not think much of the women themselves. After all, what is a ship in a bottle? Now these bottles were unbreakable. And the men could not break their women to get to the ships ...'

The old man lit his cigarette with a stick from the fire. I turned the roasting maize over: it was turning into a delicious yellow like the heart of an overpowering sunset.

He said: 'A man wakes up in a huge night and goes out to make water and is never seen again.'

He wheezed and choked on his cigarette; between gasps he told me the following: 'A man found a little egg in a small hole beside which was a massive tree shattered by lightning. When he returned home he gave the egg to his newly married wife, who loved eggs the way plants like moisture and water. She cooked and ate it. That night there was a storm. But the good couple went to bed early to make their own love-storm. Afterwards they slept in each other's arms. Then lightning spattered and stitched the black night and, as its great thunderous drum dinned upon that house, the husband dropped from the bed with a crash. The woman had also awakened. "You pushed me!" he said crossly, trying to get into the bed. "Move over!" he said more softly. "But I'm over here at this far end," she replied truthfully. He tried again. But there was something there and he couldn't get in. He became very angry, for it was cold and chilly. "I'll settle this once and for all!" he said, and lit a candle. And pushed back the blankets. There was a huge bloodstained egg there; it was still tender, as though newly laid. The woman, gaping, pushed away the rest of the bedclothes and looked down at herself: she was stretched and bloody like one who has just given birth. The man was staring like one who is listening to the wings of a curse flying overhead. And as they looked they became aware that the storm outside had come down quietly and had tiptoed into the room to listen to them.'

The old man stopped. He took a puff at his long-ashed cigarette. I drew the roasted maize from the fire, and blew the ash from them and put them on a plate to cool them a little.

'A writer drew a circle in the sand and stepping into it said "This is my novel," but the circle, leaping, cut him clean through,' he said.

And he picked up his maize and began to eat. I quickly followed his example for I love roast maize. The old man chewed slowly, savouring every droplet of sweetness.

He swallowed regretfully and said: 'An angry youth chose a spot on this little ball of Earth. And he stayed on that little spot for a long time. Waiting, I suppose; but he did not even think he was waiting. Did not believe in living long enough in one place to grow roots from his angry brains and sprout leaves from his angry mind. No. No, he just stayed there on that tiny spot. Till his eyesight cracked like a little twig and his life, withering greatly, began to glow around his remains. Years passed. The four winds howled about that spot. Lightning stitched the air. Underneath, the Earth moved as it has always moved.'

He cast at me a quick but shrewd glance.

'Don't take these things too seriously. They are the ramblings of a tramp. Just bits and pieces I picked up and pocketed.'

He said: 'A man to whom everything under the sun had really happened was walking home when he met a green dwarf who looked up at him scornfully, sneeringly. "Why do you walk with a crutch?" the dwarf asked with contempt. The man held out his hands and stamped his legs on the gravel road and said: "Can't you see I have no crutch? Indeed, I have no need of it."

But the dwarf spat on to a passing chameleon and said to the man: "You have the biggest crutch I have ever seen a cripple use."

'The man, astonished, and perhaps a little angry, demanded: "What crutch?"

'And the dwarf, spitting again at the skulking chameleon, said: "Why, your mind."

'And with that they parted. Now that road is between the

water and the earth and many have grown old and died journeying upon it. And because all men use it, that road is greatly frequented by beggars like me. One day I too chose my spot and sat upon it, waiting for the travellers to pass me by. It was Sunday and early. Soon a solid youth in a crimson jacket strolled up to me and asked if I knew where he could buy a white chicken. Do you know where I sent him? To the white soldiers' whorehouse: they beat him to a pulp. Or into a paste, I'm not sure. No one else came, and I became bored and began to scratch and look around. That is when I found this little package. That crimson-jacket character must have dropped it. There are photographs of you and your friends and little notes about what you do. Take them ... I think Trouble is knocking impatiently on our door.'

THE TRANSFORMATION OF HARRY

At last Harry rang off and came out of the phone booth. He was smiling.

'She's coming!' he said. 'I can land her any time now.'

He was speaking of Ada, Nestar's daughter. Indeed, for months he had been talking about nothing else; except the Essentials, as he put it. Harry desperately wanted not so much to make it with Ada – it could have been any other girl – but to get at the heart of the matter and grasp those Essentials by the root. He needed that organic transformation. At the same time a woman like Ada who had made it with all sorts of white hard-ons would give him the receptacle into which he could with satisfaction pour the baptismal waters. And the transformation would be complete.

He kicked the phone booth with pleasure.

'It's good, man. Damn good.'

Of course good and evil did not come into it. For Harry all that led to his success was good. Hence good was success. And to get at the heart of that divine aura was the ambition of all who would be good.

Harry knew evil. Evil was failure. There were a lot of failures where Harry came from. Uneducated shits who counted their pennies and paid the rent and made their wives pregnant for the umpteenth time and went without tobacco or beer in order to save up for a sewing machine. Calloused palms. Dirty bodies. Overalls. This was evil, failure. Toiling in factories and mines and on the roads and bridges and in farms and fields for – what? Failure.

Harry also did not think much of women. Even Ada. He despised people for whom suffering seemed to be an in-built element in life. But he liked screwing the way some people like cheating others.

As Harry walked towards his room, a stinging cloud of flies suddenly swooped upon his head and he ran like a cat whose fur is on fire. He slammed the door behind him and leaned against it to regain his breath. And then he locked it. He then released and shadowed the Venetian blinds and stooped to open his metal trunk. It was half full of *Playboy* magazines. He took out the one he wanted. She was an Afro-American model – wistful longing, waiting. Success. Harry smiled tenderly down at her and unzipped his trousers.

He felt ready for Ada. Nothing would go wrong. The moth would emerge from the flame transformed into its more angelic kin. And afterwards it would all have been a mere dream, and he would remember it as a pleasant irritation. Harry looked at his watch.

Later, as he absently chewed his dinner and with one eye and one ear looked and listened to the life around him, Harry had a premonition of success. It was a tiny spasm, blindingly delicious, as if heaven had distilled its choicest water and dipped a fine white feather into its essence and then delicately touched it to the christwound in his sphincter.

Harry did not like people who 'think too much'. They stink of failure, his father had told him. Hence Harry, after that phone call and after that thoughtful dinner, met a black detective in a' crowded beer hall and casually exchanged white envelopes with him. He then returned to the Student Union, and over a shandy waited for Ada to appear. At one point he idly took out the envelope and ran his eyes over it lovingly. Smiling. He was ready for the last rite whose performance, though a mere formality, would seal the bond of his transformation forever.

But a hand suddenly tweaked his cheek playfully.

'Hello, arse-face,' Philip greeted him, and at the same time signalled to someone in the shadow.

Ada came and sat down.

Philip tugged again – this time viciously – at Harry's cheek.

'This him, Ada?'

'Yes.'

'Let's hear it from your own lips, spyfart,' Philip said.

When Harry said nothing Philip reached down and grabbed Harry's shirtfront.

And Harry licked his lips. Philip shook him. As he did so an envelope dropped to the floor.

Harry whined: 'I've dropped something.' His voice was hoarse. He swallowed.

Ada was staring at the envelope.

Philip released him and turned: 'Would you like a drink, Ada?'

Harry shot up. But Philip, who had anticipated such a move, stuck out his foot and Harry smashed on to the floor. Philip picked up the envelope and walked over to the bar.

At this point I thought it better for all concerned for me to join that unhappy table. I did not look at Harry.

'Everything all right now, Ada?' I asked.

'Almost.'

'Harry, why don't you get out now?'

Ada smiled generously as she said: 'He tried.'

Philip returned with two gins. When he saw me he winked rather unconvincingly: 'I thought I saw you skulking about with your notebook,' he said.

'I was.'

It was good to be with Philip again.

Harry licked his bruised lips.

'May I please have my envelope back?'

But Philip dipped into his coat pocket and brought out two identical white envelopes. And held them out to Harry.

'Take your pick,' Philip said.

Harry stared and took a long gulping pull at his shandy. Harry could not bring himself to choose. To gamble. Harry, seeing failure everywhere, pleaded for a breathing space.

'Go and get another drink if you like,' Philip winked generously.

Harry rushed to the bar.

Philip turned to me.

'I see you're still using your friends to make up improbable stories,' he yawned.

And sat up with a jolt. He looked at the letters and then his eyes lit on my empty hands.

'That's it,' he cracked his fingers, 'I knew there was something wrong.'

Amused, I asked: 'What?'

Philip got up. He said: 'You don't have a drink. I'll get you one.'

He put the letters side by side on the table and walked to the bar. I had begun to wonder what it was that was eating him.

Harry returned. And could not tear his eyes away from the two letters.

Ada, unsmiling, said: 'Harry, what you're going through now is exactly what you made me suffer all these months.'

The sweat had broken out on his forehead. But, unaccountably, Harry smiled: 'Yes, but I was right. I knew it. I was right.'

And he added: 'You are quite a woman, too.'

'And what are you quite?' I asked.

'I don't know yet,' Harry said.

He seemed to be slowly coming out of a shell. Unshelling. Like a seed cracking out of its nutshell.

'I said take your pick,' Philip nudged him, and pushed in my direction the largest whisky and soda I had ever seen. He knew I hated – loathed – whisky.

I drank.

Ada shrugged, tossing off her gin. She and Philip had a sort of understanding. But Philip wanted a more conventional arrangement. And Ada did not want to deviate from what she saw was her destiny. And she was also having a bad time with her mother who was the most famous whore in the town. What she wanted to know was whether there was just so much predetermined shit in her family. And this had made her irritable of late; besides, Philip was getting more and more disgusting about their whole relationship – marriage was what he wanted. And she had known Harry's game from the first phone call. And she had asked herself: why did he pick *me* for all this bullshit? When Philip had signalled for her to join him she had desperately wanted to ask Harry: why, am I then so full of shit? But when she saw him she understood at a glance and her knowledge of him made her sick with herself. And what could she do about Philip? She could do nothing, because there was nothing about himself in her understanding of him. It made her impatient, this blindness which he was in her mind.

Philip had by this time bought a Gordon's bottle and refilled the glasses. I still had my whisky; I could not imagine any negro drinking Southern Comfort except at gunpoint.

And there we all were; in an uncertain country, ourselves uncertain. A land with a sly heart; and ourselves ready to be deceived. A morally corrosive atmosphere, and ourselves base metals ready for the -acids of maturity.

And on the table – transfixed by Harry's popping-out eyes – the two envelopes.

I could see in Harry's piercing look a monomania which could only lead to one end. I looked up hastily and, like Sancho Panza, knocked back every drop of whisky in one draught.

Philip pushed the Gordon's towards me.

Gratefully I reached out and refuelled again and again.

Where was hope – where was vision?

Something shrill tore into my eardrum.

Startled, I looked up. Philip and Ada were also staring.

The maddening high-pitched needles were coming from Harry.

But he was not making any sound.

THE SLOW SOUND OF HIS FEET

But someday if I sit
Quietly at this corner listening, there
May come this way the slow sound of his feet.
                    J. D. C. Pellow

I dreamt last night that the Prussian surgeon Johann Friedrich Dieffenbach had decided that I stuttered because my tongue was too large; and he cut my large organ down to size by snipping off chunks from the tip and the sides. Mother woke me up to tell me that father had been struck down by a speeding car at the roundabout; I went to the mortuary to see him, and they had sewn back his head to the trunk and his eyes were open. I tried to close them but they would not shut, and later we buried him with his eyes still staring upward.

It was raining when we buried him.

It was raining when I woke up looking for him. His pipe lay where it had always been, on the mantelpiece. When I looked at it the rain came down strongly and rattled the tin roof of my memories of him. His leatherbound books were upright and very still in the bookcase. One of them was Oliver Bloodstein's *A Handbook on Stuttering*. There was also a cuneiform tablet – a replica of the original – on which was written, several centuries before Christ, an earnest prayer for release from the anguish of stuttering. He had told me that Moses, Demosthenes, and Aristotle also had a speech impediment; that Prince Battus, advised by the oracle, cured himself of stuttering by conquering the North Africans; and that Demosthenes taught himself to speak without blocks by outshouting the surf through a mouthful of pebbles.

It was still raining when I lay down and closed my eyes, and

108

I could see him stretched out in the sodden grave and trying to move his mandibles. When I woke up I could feel him inside me; and he was trying to speak, but I could not. Aristotle muttered something about my tongue being abnormally thick and hard. Hippocrates then forced my mouth open and stuck blistering substances to my tongue to drain away the dark fluid. Celsus shook his head and said: 'All that the tongue needs is a good gargle and a massage.' But Galen, who would not be left out, said my tongue was merely too cold and wet. And Francis Bacon suggested a glass of hot wine.

As I walked down to the beer hall I saw a long line of troop-carriers drawn up at the gates of the township. They were all white soldiers. One of them jumped down and prodded me with his rifle and demanded to see my papers. I had only my University student card. He scrutinised it for such a long time that I wondered what was wrong with it.

'Why are you sweating?' he asked.

I took out my paper and pencil and wrote something and showed it to him.

'Dumb, eh?'

I nodded.

'And you think I'm dumb too, eh?'

I shook my head. But before I could finish shaking my head, his hand came up fast and smacked my jaw. I brought up my hand to wipe away the blood, but he blocked it and hit me again. My false teeth cracked and I was afraid I would swallow the jagged fragments. I spat them out without bringing up my hand to my mouth.

'False teeth too, eh?'

My eyes were stinging. I couldn't see him clearly. But I nodded.

'False identity too, eh?'

I had an overwhelming desire to move my jaws and force

my tongue to repeat what my student card had told him. But I only managed to croak out unintelligible sounds. I pointed to my paper and pencil which had fallen to the ground.

He nodded.

But as I bent down to pick them up, he brought up his knee suddenly and almost broke my neck.

'Looking for a stone, were you, eh?'

I shook my head and it hurt so much I couldn't stop shaking my head any more. There were running feet behind me; my mother's and my sister's voices. There was the sharp report of firing. Mother, struck in mid-stride, her body held rigid by the acrid air, was staring straight through her eyes. A second later, something broke inside her and she toppled over. My sister's outstretched hand, coming up to touch my face, flew to her opening mouth and I could feel her straining her vocal muscles to scream through my mouth.

Mother died in the ambulance.

The sun was screaming soundlessly when I buried her. There were hot and cold rings around its wet brightness. My sister and I, we walked the four miles back home, passing the African's Only hospital, the Europeans Only hospital, the British South Africa Police camp, the Post Office, the railway station, and walked across the mile-wide green belt, and walked into the black township.

The room was so silent I could feel it trying to move its tongue and its mandibles, trying to speak to me. I was staring up at the wooden beams of the roof. I could hear my sister pacing up and down in her room which was next to mine. I could feel her strongly inside me. My room contained nothing but my iron bed, my desk, my books, and the canvases upon which I had for so long tried to paint the feeling of the silent but desperate voices inside me. I stung back the tears and felt her so strongly inside me I could not bear it. But the door mercifully opened and they came in leading her by the hand. She was dressed in pure white. A pale blue light was emanating from her. On her slender feet were the sandals of gleaming white leather. But the magnet of her fleshless face, the two empty eye-sockets, the sharp grinning teeth (one of her teeth was slightly chipped), the high cheekbones, and the cruelly missing nose – the magnet of them held my gaze until, it seemed, my straining eyes were abruptly sucked into her rigid stillness.

He was dressed in black. Her fleshless hand lay still in his fleshless fingers. His head had not been sewn back properly; it was precariously leaning to one side and it seemed as if it would fall off any moment. His skull had a jagged crack running down from the centre of the forehead to the tip of the lower jaw; the skull had been crudely welded back into shape, so much so it looked as though it would fall apart any moment.

The pain in my eyes was unbearable. I blinked. When I opened my eyes they had gone. My sister was standing in their place. She was breathing heavily and that made my chest ache. I held out my hand and touched her: she was warm and alive and her very breath was painfully anxious in my voice. I had to speak! But before I could utter a single sound she bent down over me and kissed me. The hot flush of it shook us in each other's arms. Outside, the night was making a muffled gibberish upon the roof and the wind had tightened its hold upon the windows. We could hear, in the distance, the brass and strings of a distant military band.

I had never killed a goat before. But it was Christmas. And father who had always done it was dead. He had been dead for seven years. My sister, Ruth, could not possibly be expected to kill the goat. It was supposed to be a man's job. And mother was dead too. There were the two of us in the house, Ruth and I. I was on sabbatical from the university and Christmas would, I had hoped, be a break from the book I was writing. But there had to be a goat to spoil everything. Actually it was Christmas Eve, and that was the time of killing and skinning the goat. Everybody in the township would be killing their own family goat. While I tried to find an excuse to get out of having to kill the goat myself, I reminded Ruth that a goat was a passionate creature beloved of Pan and how could I kill that beast in me? I was, I said, myself a hardy, lively, wanton, horned and bearded ruminant quadruped – if not in fact, at least in spirit. I had always been wicked. I was up there in the sky with Capricorn, I said. If all this isn't convincing, I said, what about that all important Tropic of Capricorn which seemed to make those who lived close to it vicious, nasty, spoilt, bloody Boers, and in short to kill the goat would be to disrespect a substantial part of the human extremities and interiorities. Besides, I added, you know I can't eat what I have killed. Also I was mere goat's wool in the general fabric of this great fiction we call life and could not logically be capable of such a monstrosity as murdering a poor old goat. Imagine a large assembly of bloodthirsty Germans shouting '*Geist*' at a terrified little Jewish boy. All this mass-extermination of perfectly harmless but god-created goats seemed to me to be nothing but a distortion of what Christmas was really about. Which was? Which was? Well, we're Africans anyway and all this nonsense about Christmas was merely a sordid distraction. After all, I said, aren't whites and blacks skinning each other now ready for the Christmas pot, lugging each other by the heels into the universal kitchen to dress each one up with chillies and mustard and black pepper and 'chips and afterwards everybody would pat their stomachs and belch gently and scratch their bellies in which the feeling of Freedom and Christmas was being slowly digested. The whole business of expressing Christian glee by cutting the throats of much-maligned goats was indeed sickening, not to mention the so-called domestication of goats in concentration-camp-style kraals when what could be more majestic and courageous and rugged than pure mountain goats? I could not for the life of me see anything but inhumanity in buying a goat for a few shillings and tethering it to an old barbed-wire fence and having babies watch its throat and guts being cut up. Besides, I was not a real killer at all. Perhaps sometimes I inadvertently stepped on a beetle that was not watching where it was going, and of course I did murder all those damned mosquitoes that were plaguing my rooms at the university, and that nasty fat fly which so maddened me that I took a swipe at it with a hardback *Complete Shakespeare*. I think I only grazed its compound eyes and chucked it into the waste-paper basket and then the crafty insect played so hard at being dead it actually died. I agree that snake which was skulking around in the apple tree when you were looking longingly at the red-ripest one probably did not deserve to be scared to death by my shotgun. And every self-respecting pimply boy had a rubber sling to stone birds to death. And fighting is not a different business: you raise your fist at somebody and at once you are a potential killer – there is nothing manly in that. This business about 'being a real man' is what is driving all of us crazy. I'll have none of it. There's nothing different between you and me except what's hanging between our legs. And if you want goat meat, kill it yourself. If I'm supposed to become a 'real man' in the twinkling of an eye by cutting the human throats of these human goats, then

I don't see why you shouldn't suddenly become a 'real woman' by the same horrible atrocity. How can you ever possibly look any living thing in the eye after becoming a grown-up by cutting the throat of a living being? What I mean is, my mind is in such a mess because every step eats up the step before it and where will this grand staircase of everything eating everything else lead us to? Who wants to be the first step and who will be the last all-eating step? God? I know that goat has probably exterminated a lot of cowering grass, and the grass itself ate up the salt and the water in the earth, and the salt and the water probably came from stinking corpses in the ground, and the corpses probably ate up something else – I mean, what the hell! At least we have got that within us which does not kill when all the bloody world out there is killing. Look, you're my sister, so don't rush me – at least give me a chance. This is not a guerrilla band from which a man cannot desert alive. It isn't Smith's army either. It's me. Me. And I'm just goat's wool that nobody can see. The way the goat is staring at me is making me nervous. But that's natural; how would you stare at people who were, in your presence, openly discussing the subject of doing away with you, skinning you and dressing you up so that you'd not be even a corpse but something good to eat, which would an hour later come out of their arses and be flushed away into a labyrinth of sewers? I know we can't eat air or stone or fire, but we can at any rate drink water. But why do we have to eat and drink at all? Whoever created us had a nasty mind! How would you feel if somebody skinned you and then hung out your skin to dry and made a pair of shoes out of it? I mean, there's people out there who'd boil your very bones to make fertiliser – and if your bones are not good enough, they boil them again and make glue out of them and give it to little schoolkids to paste up their paperdolls and stick them on a time chart that's supposed to explain how human civilisation worked out from the Neanderthal to the man of today who is supposed

114

to see things like a camera lens looks at you just before the shutter falls. I refuse to see things that way! They look at you like you want me to look at that goat. They look at you like you were a potential meal, and they digest your innards and fart you out and call it progress. It terrifies me the way we are capable of imprisoning whole populations of pigs, cattle, poultry, goats and sheep and fatten them up and then herd them into gas chambers and when they are dead strip them of their flesh and bones and brains and gold teeth and marriage rings and spectacles – strip them of everything and call it what, intensive farming, modern progress. And we call it everything else but exactly what it is. The world was not created to serve for a meal for us. If it was, then God help the likes of me. God? It's his Christmas and in 1915 and 1916 on the Western Front they took a break from shooting each other up and pushed a football about and then as soon as his holy birthday was over they began blasting the tonsils out of each other again. One of the bloody Germans was a clown with a goldfish. I don't want to be a goldfish in somebody's idea of a cosmic farce. The goat doesn't want to be either. And that poor archbishop in Uganda probably did not want to be a goldfish in Amin's head, either. And probably the goldfish would prefer it if I left its name out of this.

Heavens! it's so late already. What time is supper? What do you mean, I'll have to kill the goat if I want any supper? I want my supper. This is the first time I've been able to come home in seven years, and would you deny me a humble repast? The goat? Him? He is really the humble repast, is he? Then – God help me – I'll ... Let's give him to those starving Makonis. They probably haven't had anything again today. Hey – look out! it's broken its tether. See how it runs, like Pan himself, or like a scapegoat, or like me when I was younger. It's burst through that crowd! It's in the forest! Well, good luck to you, Pan. Don't look so offended, Ruth, because we are eating out. I've reserved the table already.

At that posh place, Brett's. My wife will be joining us there in – let's see – five minutes. You two have got a lot to talk about – it's been seven years, you know. I just hope I won't be booked for speeding.

BURNING IN THE RAIN

The mirror, I suppose, was at the heart of it. It was full length. He would stand before it naked, and study himself slyly. There was a certain ridiculousness about the human body which he could not accept in himself. He loved to mock the body in the mirror, mock it obliquely like a child who fears adult retaliation.

And then the mirror settled deep in his mind and things became rather ominous.

The ape in the mirror got the better of him. But he would retaliate by dressing himself from head to foot. However, the eyes and part of the face ... Those hairy hands and the backs of his hands where those scars ... Monster!

He rushed out into the rain the way some people find refuge in tears of self-pity. The whitewashed barrack-like houses squatted gloomily on both sides of the gravel street. Above him the sky's mind was full of black and angry thoughts and would flash suddenly with the brilliance of a childlike insight.

He reached Number 191.

Frank answered the door.

Frank's small, sharply angled face hinted at the existence of things tainted but sweet. The boy thought him a fool – and now shouted: 'Margaret! You're wanted.'

Margaret came.

She was tall and soft and smelled of the good things of the rain – little fists of budding leaves and the heady scent of an old golden time. But she was delicate, like a taboo which one is reluctant to name. And she was unhappy. She worried about that mirror of his. And she wanted to break it, name it exactly to his face and watch the glass of it splinter away, and his face settle back once more into the gentle lines she had once known.

He could hear the howling of a baby as he kissed her.

Once more he wondered how and by what alchemy she had been conceived out of such squalor.

'Margaret! Bring the visitor inside,' her grandmother shouted.

'We're just going! It's almost time for it to start, and we'll be late if … ' she shouted back but was interrupted by a knowing jeer: 'Whore!'

They fled into the rain, dodged the barren apple tree which stood in the yard like a symbol, and walked slowly up the gravel street. The rain came down in little liquid rocks which broke on their heads with a gentleness too rapid to be anything other than overpowering. She laughed a laugh that had little sharp teeth in it and it warmed them, this biting intimacy with the rain. Drops of God's water, that's what rain was. Out of its secret came the leaves of a life worth living. But out of it too came the gorgeous images of the mirror which would not be broken.

They had, that summer, gone to swim in the river. The river gods had been generous and she had felt their blessing trembling upon her skin as she surfaced and shook the crystal-clear water from her shining eyes. He too had dived a deep breathtaking dive at the deepest side where the manfish lived. He had – at long last! – broken the surface and emerged sucking in great armfuls of breath, laughing and beating the silver shimmering lattices around him. At the head of the stream, that's where they had, with great violence, fused into one and it was among the petunias so unbearably sweet that they had become afraid and listened to the staring motionless thing which made the rivers flow. The rushing rapids of them had crashed onwards into the Indian Ocean. If only life was like that always and, yes, one did not have to see the reflections of one's own thoughts. If one was rock. A great breaking spray of it sparked by rainbows. But the frost of the mirror chilled everything into the ice of reproachful silences. It made her see herself in him and realise there was nothing on the other side. Only a great mind-bending emptiness, that other side. The worst of deaths. And then work, work'. She worked as a nanny to a Mrs Hendriks who was fat and soft-voiced and suspected her of numerous but vague sins. Sin. Her first sin was with him behind a hedge. She had stared upwards over his shoulder and watched the great slice of moon big and round and gleaming white. She had not wondered what lay behind it all. On that other side. His face, so close to hers, was utterly strange. Incredible. And she wondered what it was in him that was touching her lips. And the tears coldly stung out of her eyes. Burning. He licked them from her cheeks, and the pain of it stained his eyes like a child punishing itself for some short-coming. Was she the punishment for the ape in the mirror?

It was wet and warm, this feeling of the rain.

The train had chugged furiously into the night, flashing its great beam. They had packed their things hurriedly and in the taxi they had watched the burning street-lights which shone brightly like the guardians of an obsessive barrenness. It had been, in the train, crowded and hot and dozy and they had talked endlessly of the soul of the country, how painful and lovely and boring it all was, hurtling on into God's shadow.

The illusion of going somewhere.

That was his childhood, that illusion. But time had rubbed pepper into his eyes and the stinging of it had maddened it out of him. The mirror said it all and in it he knew his kinsman; the ape, lumbering awkwardly into his intimacy. He had looked behind it all and seen the huge emptiness of it. But the depth in the mirror looked more real. More substantial than the discontent gleaming and humming around his head. Though the thought of what now lay in the ancient graveclothes tormented him, the least it had to say stung him into activity. He had been happy, unbearably happy, as a child. But at the threshold of manhood he had lingered uneasily; reluctant to take that irrevocable step.

119

The ape in the mirror had laughed sarcastically and had danced and trampled it all into at best a doubtful outcome. But he had stood his ground and smiled a tiny diamond smile. Was this all there was to it? This eternal gnawing in the gut. Racking, always, one's brains in the doorway. Remembering sharply the faces but being unable to stick names to them. And when a name stuck he invariably forgot the face it belonged to. What frightened him was he could never recognise his own face – especially after an encounter with the ape in the mirror. And the ape, knowing its power over him, gradually made the encounters more sordid, more unbearable. It left him feeling like a piece of cloth that has been dipped into cold water and then wrung out to dry on the clothesline of a precarious sanity. This happened frequently – until he began to forget things.

At first it was a matter of losing a few hours. But he began to miss out whole days. And when he came out of those blank pages it would be without the faintest recollection of where he had been or what he had done – but invariably he would not even know that he had been in a blackout. The first instance he became aware of something going wrong was when he woke out of a deep sleep to find himself still fully dressed and covered all over with soot – from head to toe, soot. And his knees and knuckles were bruised – his right cheek caked with blood. And there was a red bag in the middle of the room and it was full of obscene Christmas cards. At first he could make nothing of it all.

The second time, though equally disturbing, was less painful; he woke up to find that he had painted himself with whitewash and was wearing a European wig. It took him hours to get rid of the paint and for days afterwards he reeked of nothing else. It made him more than uneasy: something was definitely getting out of hand. The ape in the mirror seemed excited; excitable; it seemed to be treasuring a huge but secret joke at his expense. His gloom deepened. He was really worried that though definitely something was going on he could himself feel nothing at all; he was not sick, had never had nightmares, had never had a nervous breakdown. In fact felt new, like new wine, healthy and supremely fit.

And then he woke up to find his room in great disorder, as though a fiend had been let loose in it. The only thing that had not been touched was the mirror. Everything else had been ripped up, smashed, torn up and flung about. The room reeked of human faeces; there were mounds of it smeared everywhere ... even on the ceiling.

He groaned. It took him six days to clean the mess up. And on the seventh he rested. He was sitting in the armchair when there was a knock on the door. Margaret came in. Immediately she crinkled her nose at the smell of the room; it was unmistakable – something tainted yet sweet. An impure honey scent. And there was a hint of wet petunias in it. She asked him what it was; and for the first time he told her lies. Lies. She seemed to divine it in him. She knew it was the mirror talking to her. And she could not stand it. She casually picked up an empty bottle from the little table and flung it. It splintered into a thousand tiny mirrors – but did not break apart. It simply shivered into a thousand minute lenses glinting into her being. And he in the armchair had changed with it; he laughed bitterly. There was a row; their first real argument. And for the first time they swore at each other.

'You fucking bitch!'

'Shit!'

'Up your arse!'

'Fucking shit!'

And she burst into tears. It had all been so sudden.

Now the little rocks of rain crushed faster upon them like a child tugging for attention. The whitewashed houses on either side of the street seemed to have changed, too, to have become slightly menacing. Slightly evil. And the pattering of the rain sounded like the microscopic commotion of six million little people fleeing a national catastrophe.

Shivering at it, their arms tightened about each other.

PROTISTA

There was a great drought in our region. All the rivers dried up. All the wells dried up. There was not a drop of water anywhere. I lived alone in a hut next to the barren fig-tree which had never been known to have any fruit on it. Now and then it would show signs of being alive but these always withered and were carried away by the relentless winds from the south-east which were dry and dusty and would sting into the very coolness of our minds. Those winds, they were fierce and scathing and not a drop of moisture was left.

My hut was on a slight rise on the shoulder of the Lesapi Valley. The valley was red and clayey and scarred with drought fissures from the burning sun and the long cold nights when I lay awake thinking of Maria the huntress who had one morning taken down her bows and arrows and had gone out into the rising sun and had never been seen again. But before she left she had drawn a circle in red chalk on the wall by my bed and said: 'If the circle begins to bleed and run down the wall that means I am in danger. But if it turns blue and breaks up into a cross then that means I am coming home.'

The drought began the very day she left me. There was not a green blade of grass left. There was not a green leaf of hope left; the drought had raised its great red hand and gathered them all and with one hot breath had swept all the leaves into a red dot on the pencil-line of the horizon where Maria had last been seen taking aim with her bow and arrow at a running gazelle.

And twelve long lean years had passed by somehow.

I still had three more years to serve. I had been exiled to this raw region by a tribunal which had found me guilty of various political crimes. Maria had been my secretary and my wife and had for long endured the barren fire of exile with me. And the sun burnt each year to cinders that darkened the aspect of the region. I began to forget things. My dreams still clung defiantly to the steel wire of old memories which I no longer had the power to arrange clearly in my mind. My imagination was constantly seared by the thought of water, of thirst, of dying barren and waterless and in the grave to be nothing but dehydrated 'remains'. It was not so much forgetting as being constantly preoccupied with the one image of water. And water in my mind was inextricably involved with my thoughts about Maria, about my own impotence, about the fig-tree, and about the red soil of the Lesapi Valley. The years of my life that had gone were so much time wasted, so little done, so many defeats, so little accomplished; they were years I would have preferred to forget if they did not in themselves contain my youth and the only time Maria and I had been happy together. And now, disjointed, disconnected, they came back to me unexpectedly and with such a new grain in them that I hardly recognised them for what they were. There was the story my father had told me, when I was barely six years of age, about the resilience of human roots: a youth rebelling against the things of his father had one morning fled from home and had travelled to the utmost of the earth where he was so happy that he wrote on their wall the words 'I have been here' and signed his new name after the words; the years rolled by with delight until he tired of them and thought to return home and tell his father about them. But when he neared home his father, who was looking out for him, met him and said, 'All this time you thought you were actually away from me, you have been right here in my palm.' And the father opened his clenched hand and showed the son what was written in this hand. The words – and the very same signature – of the son were clearly written in the father's open palm: 'I have been here.' The son was so stunned and angry that he there and then slew his father and hung himself on a barren fig-tree which stood in the garden. I dreamed of this

124

story many times, and each time some detail of it would change into something else. At times the father would become Maria the huntress; the son would be myself; and the fig-tree would become the tree just outside my own hut. But sometimes the son would become Maria and I would be the father whose clenched hand contained everything that Maria was.

The scarred hand of exile was dry and deathlike and the lines of its palm were the waterless riverbeds, the craters and fissures and dry channels scoured out of the earth by the relentless drought. My own hands, with their scars and calluses and broken fingernails, sometimes seemed to belong not to me but to this exacting punishment of exile. And yet they had once tenderly held Maria to me; and she had been soft and warm and wild and demanding in these very same hands. These hands that now were part of the drought, they had once cupped the quickening liquids of life, the hearty laughter of youth, the illusory security of sweet-smelling illusions. These hands that now were so broken, they had once tried to build and build and build a future out of the bricks of the past and of the present. These hands that had never touched the cheek of a child of my own, they were now utterly useless in the slow-burning furnace of the drought whose coming had coincided with Maria's going away from me.

Her arms were long and thin and the fingers were long and finely moulded though her nails, like mine, had long since lost their natural lustre and had become broken and jagged. And she was gentle, fiercely so, for she knew her great strength. She was a head taller than I and her long full legs sometimes outstrode me when we went out for a walk in the Lesapi Valley. I had named the valley Lesapi after my birthplace where once I had learned to fish, to swim and to lie back into the soft green grass and relax, with my eyes closed and my head ringing with the cawing of the crows and the leisurely moo of cows grazing on Mr Robert's side of the river, where it was fenced and there was a notice about trespassers. And in the summer the white people held rubber-boat races on the river and sometimes I was allowed to watch them swirling along in the breezy hold of the river. But somebody drowned one day and my father told me not to go down to the river any more because the drowned boy would have turned into a manfish and he would want to have company in the depths of the waters. Water was good, but only when it did not have a manfish in it. My first nightmare was about a white manfish which materialised in my room and licked its great jaws at me and came towards my bed and said: 'Come, come, come with me', and it raised its hand and drew a circle on the wall behind my head and said, 'That circle will always bleed until you come to me.' I looked at his hand and the fingers were webbed, with livid skin attaching each finger to another finger. And then he stretched out his index finger and touched my cheek with it. It was like being touched by a red-hot spike; and I cried out, but I could not hear my own voice: and they were trying to break down the door, and I cried out louder and the wooden door splintered apart and father rushed in with a world war in his eyes. But the manfish had gone; and there was a black frog squatting where he had been. The next day the medicine-man came and examined me and shook his head and said that an enemy had done it. He named Barbara's father, and my father bought strong medicine which would make what had been done to me boomerang on Barbara's father. They then made little incisions on my face and on my chest and rubbed a black powder into them, and said that should I ever come near water I must say to myself: 'Help me, grandfather.' My grandfather was dead, but they said that his spirit was always looking and watching over me. They made a fire and cast the black frog into it, and the medicine man said he would seed its ashes in Barbara's father's garden. But he could do nothing about the circle on the wall, because although I could clearly see it no one else could. Shortly after this, my eyes dimmed a little and I have had to wear spectacles since then; at the time, however, it only made the little circle jump sharply at me each time I entered my room. The spot where the manfish had touched me swelled with pus, and mother had to boil water with lots of salt and then squeeze the pus out and bathe it with the salted water; after that it healed a little, and ever since I have always had a little black mark there on my face. Soon afterwards Barbara's father went mad and one day his body was fished out of the river by police divers who wore black fishsuits. There were various abrasions on his face and the body was utterly naked, and something in the river seemed to have tried to eat him – there were curious toothmarks on his buttocks and his shoulders had been partially eaten; the hands looked as though something had chewed them and tried to gnaw them from the arms.

Every morning, when the sun rose, there was a fine mist in the valley, and the interplay of the sun's rays on it created fantastic images within the mist. And they invariably looked like people I had once known. The shapes within the mist were somewhat formless, and yet with such a realistic solidity to them that I could never quite decide what to think. I had named the valley to give it the myths and faces of moments in my own life. But as the years went by, the waterless valley – paralysed by the cramping effects of an overwhelming oppression – emitted its own symbolic mists which overpowered my own imagination, and at last so erupted with its own smoke and fire and faces and shapes that I could not tell which valley was the real Lesapi. I had been physically weakened by the great shortage of water and the shortage of food. Besides, I had never been very strong. And this eerie region which was so stricken by the sun seemed to have a prodigious population of insects: flies, mosquitoes, cicadas, spiders and scorpions. The cicadas were good to eat; the rest tormented me with their sudden stinging. The massive difference between the temperature of the days and the temperature of the nights was also a severe torture. And the manner in which I had been brought up was not calculated to cramp and stifle the imagination; rather my imagination has always been quick to the point of frightening me. All this made the valley come out alive at my very doorstep. The circle which Maria had drawn on the wall seemed alive; it was in constant motion, changing colour, breaking and rearranging itself into a cross, moving again into a circle and bleeding and running down the wall till I cried in my sleep. It seemed I was in many places at one and the same time; my sleeping and waking had no difference between them. There was a sharp but remote flame of pain inside my head; it seemed I was not so much talking to myself as talking to the things of that valley.

I woke up one morning and at once felt in myself that something was wrong. I could not move; I could move neither my body nor my hands nor my feet. At first I thought something had in the night strapped me down to the ground, but I could feel no bonds binding me. When I realised what had happened I almost cried out – but held my breath because there was no one to hear me. Not only had my hair grown into the floor like roots, but also my fingers and my toes and the veins and arteries of my body had all in my sleep grown into the earth floor. I have been turned into some sort of plant, I thought. And as soon as that thought seared through my head I immediately could feel that my skin had turned into bark. It has happened at last, I said to myself. As I did so I noticed that the circle on the wall had begun to bleed and was running down the wall: something had happened to Maria. I could not feel my eyes, nor my ears, but, strangely, I could see and I could hear. I do not know how long I lay there; nor what days or weeks passed as I lay there fighting back the feverish delirium that soon swamped me. And I was staring fixedly at Maria's life bleeding on the wall; and stared at it so much that I could see nothing else but that red circle bleeding slowly down the wall.

It was like sleeping with one's eyes open.

The footsteps outside had stopped at my door and I could hear heavy breathing. The roof rattled a little as the south-east wind swept by. And then the breathing stopped. The wind stopped too, and the roof did not rattle any more. It suddenly dawned on me that the footsteps were actually inside me; they were my old heart beating, my old things come home. The door had not opened, but I could see her clearly. She was mere bones, a fleshless skeleton, and she was sitting on a tree-trunk. I was the tree-trunk. I do not know how long she sat there. She was weeping; clear tears, silvery and yet like glass, coming out of the stone of her eyeless sockets; and her small gleaming head rested in the open bones of her palms, whose arms rested lightly on her knees. And she held between her front teeth a silver button which I recognised: I had years before bought her a coat which had buttons like that. It was the sight of her forlornly chewing that button which filled me with such a great sadness that I did not realise that my roots had been painlessly severed and that what was left to do was to bind my wounds and once more – but with a fresh eye – walk the way of the valley. The roof was rattling once more; the south-east winds were singing a muffled song through the door. And those horrid footfalls retreated until their distant echo beat silently in my breast.

After that, the sun never came up. I do not know where it had decided to go. Perhaps it fell into the sea where the great manfish lives. Anyway, the night did not come either; it had retreated to the bedrock of the deepest sea where the great manfish came from. There was in the sky so much of its face that even the stars had grown vicious and turned into menfish. And they all wanted company; they were all hungry for me, thirsty for me. But I kept a careful watch and always chewed the silver button, because that alone can keep them away.

Yesterday I met Barbara's father in the valley.

'I'll get you in the end, you rascal!' he screamed.

But I bit the silver button and turned myself into a crocodile and laughed my great sharp teeth at him.

He instantly turned himself into mist, and I could only bite chunks of air.

While I was cursing him, a voice I did not recognise said: 'You thought it was all politics, didn't you?'

But there was no one there.

I sneered: 'Isn't it?'

And I sullenly turned myself back into human shape. I had decided to write all this down because I do not know when the stinking menfish will get me. Maria, if ever you find this – my head is roaring with fever and I scarcely know what I have written – I think the menfish are out to undermine my reason – if ever you find this – I think Barbara's father is coming to get me and the sky and the earth and the air are all full of monsters like him and me – like him – I wish I had been able to give you a child – my head! – all grown-ups are menfish, but remember perhaps there is still a chance that the children – my head!

I have been a manfish all my life. Maria, you did well to leave me. I must go.

BLACK SKIN WHAT MASK

My skin sticks out a mile in all the crowds around here. Every time I go out I feel it tensing up, hardening, torturing itself. It only relaxes when I am in shadow, when I am alone, when I wake up early in the morning, when I am doing mechanical actions, and, strangely enough, when I am angry. But it is coy and self-conscious when I draw in my chair and begin to write.

It is like a silent friend: moody, assertive, possessive, callous – sometimes.

I had such a friend once. He finally slashed his wrists. He is now in a lunatic asylum. I have since asked myself why he did what he did, but I still cannot come to a conclusive answer.

He was always washing himself – at least three baths every day. And he had all sorts of lotions and deodorants to appease the thing that had taken hold of him. He did not so much wash as scrub himself until he bled.

He tried to purge his tongue too, by improving his English and getting rid of any accent from the speaking of it. It was painful to listen to him, as it was painful to watch him trying to scrub the blackness out of his skin.

He did things to his hair, things which the good lord never intended any man to do to his hair.

He bought clothes, whole shops of them. If clothes make the man, then certainly he was a man. And his shoes were the kind that make even an elephant lightfooted and elegant. The animals that were murdered to make those shoes must have, turned in their graves and said Yeah, man.

But still he was dissatisfied. He had to have every other African within ten miles of his person follow his example. After all, if one chimpanzee learns not only to drink tea but also to promote that tea on TV, what does it profit it if all the other

131

God-created chimpanzees out there continue to scratch their fleas and swing around on their tails chittering about Rhodes and bananas?

However, he was nice enough to put it more obliquely to me one day. We were going to the New Year Ball in Oxford Town Hall.

'Don't you ever change those jeans?' he asked.

'They're my only pair,' I said.

'What do you do with your money, man, booze?'

'Yes,' I said searching through my pockets. Booze and paper and ink. The implements of my trade.

'You ought to take more care of your appearance, you know. We're not monkeys.'

'I'm all right as I am.'

I coughed and because he knew what that cough meant he tensed up as though for a blow.

'If you've got any money,' I said firmly, 'lend me a fiver.'

That day he was equally firm: 'Neither a lender nor a borrower be,' he quoted.

And then as an afterthought he said: 'We're the same size. Put on this other suit. You can have it if you like. And the five pounds.'

That is how he put it to me. And that is how it was until he slashed his wrists.

But there was more to it than that.

Appearances alone – however expensive – are doubtful climbing-boots when one hazards the slippery slopes of social adventure. Every time he opened his mouth he made himself ridiculous. Logic – that was his magic word: but unfortunately that sort of thing quickly bored even the most thick-skinned anthropologist-in-search-of-African attitudes. I was interested in the booze first and then lastly in the company. But he – God help me – relied on politics to get on with people. But who in that company in their right mind gives a shit about Rhodesia? He could never understand this.

And Christ! when it came to dancing he really made himself look a monkey. He always assumed that if a girl accepted his request for a dance it meant that she had in reality said Yes to being groped, squeezed, kissed and finally screwed off the dance floor. And the girls were quite merciless with him. The invitations would stop and all would be a chilly silence.

I did not care for the type of girl who seemed to interest him. He liked them starched, smart and demure, and with the same desperate conversation: 'What's your college ?'

'——.What's yours'?'

'——.'

Pause.

'What's your subject?'

'——.What's yours?'

'——.'

Pause. Cough.

'I'm from Zimbabwe.'

'What's that?'

'Rhodesia.'

'Oh. I'm from London. Hey (with distinct lack of interest), Smith's a bastard, isn't he?'

And he eagerly: 'As a matter of fact, I have just addressed the Africa Society on the thesis that Ian Smith blah blah blah blah blah blah blah ...'

(Yawning) 'Interesting. Very interesting.'

'Smith blah blah blah blah blah blah ... (Suddenly) Would you like to dance?'

Startled: 'Well ... I ... yes, why not.'

And that's how it was. Yes, that's how it was, until he slashed his wrists.

But there was more to it than that.

133

A black tramp accosted him one night as we walked to the University Literary Society party. It was as if he had been touched by a leper. He literally cringed away from the man, who incidentally knew me from a previous encounter when he and I had sat Christmas Eve through on a bench in Carfax drinking a bottle of whisky.

He was apopletic with revulsion and at the party could talk of nothing else: 'How can a black man in England let himself become a bum? There is much to be done. Especially in Southern Africa. What I would like to see blah blah blah ...'

'Have a drink,' I suggested.

He took it the way God accepts anything from Satan.

'You drink too much, you know,' he sighed.

'You drink too little for your own good,' I said.

The incident of the tramp must have gnawed him more than I had thought because when we got back in college he couldn't sleep and came into my room with a bottle of claret which I was glad to drink with him until breakfast when he did stop talking about impossible black bastards; he stopped talking because he fell asleep in his chair.

And that's how it was until he slashed his wrists.

But there were other sides to the story.

For example: he did not think that one of his tutors 'liked' him.

'He doesn't have to like anyone,' I pointed out, 'and neither do you.'

But he wasn't listening. He cracked his fingers and said: 'I'll send him a Christmas and New Year card, the best money can buy.'

'Why not spend the money on a Blue Nun?' I suggested.

The way he looked at me, I knew I was losing a friend.

For example: he suggested one day that if the Warden or any of the other tutors asked me if I was his friend I was to say no.

'Why?' I asked.

'You do drink too much, you know,' he said looking severe, 'and I'm afraid you do behave rather badly, you know. For instance, I heard about an incident in the beer cellar and another in the dining room and another in Cornmarket where the police had to be called, and another on your staircase ...'

I smiled.

'I'll have your suit laundered and sent up to your rooms,' I said firmly, 'and I did give you that five pounds back. So that's all right. Are you dining in Hall, because if you are then I will not, it'd be intolerable. Imagine it. We're the only two Africans in this college. How can we possibly avoid each other, or for that matter ...'

He twisted his brow. Was it pain? He had of late begun to complain of insomnia and headaches, and the lenses of his spectacles did not seem to fit the degree of his myopia. Certainly something cracked in his eyes, smarting.

'Look, I say, what, forget what I said. I don't care what they think. It's my affair, isn't it, who I choose to be friends with?'

I looked him squarely in the eye: 'Don't let them stuff bullshit into you. Or spew it out right in their faces. But don't ever puke their gut-rot on me.'

'Let's go play tennis,' he said after a moment.

'I can't. I have to collect some dope from a guy the other end of town,' I said.

'Dope? You take that – stuff?'

'Yes. The Lebanese variety is the best piss for me.'

He really was shocked.

He turned away without another word. I stared after him, hoping he wouldn't work himself up into telling his moral tutor – who was actually the one who didn't like him. And that's how it was. That's how it was, until he slashed his wrists.

But there had to be another side to it: sex.

135

The black girls in Oxford – whether African, West Indian or American – despised those of us who came from Rhodesia. After all, we still haven't won our independence. After all, the papers say we are always quarrelling among ourselves. And all the other reasons which black girls choose to believe. It was all quite unflattering. We had become – indeed we are – the Jews of Africa, and nobody wanted us. It's bad enough to have white shits despising us; but it's a more maddening story when one kettle ups its nose at another kettle ... And this he had to learn.

I didn't care one way or the other. Booze was better than girls, even black girls. And dope was heaven. But he worried. And he got himself all mixed up about a West Indian girl who worked in the kitchen. Knowing him as I did, such a 'comedown' was to say the least shattering.

'But we're all black,' he insisted.

It was another claret being drunk until breakfast.

'You might as well say to a National Front thug that we're all human,' I said.

'Maybe black men are not good enough for them,' he protested. 'Maybe all they do is dream all day long of being screwed nuts by white chaps. Maybe ...'

'I hear you've been hanging around the kitchen every day.'

He sat up.

I *was* finally losing a friend.

But he chose to sigh tragically, and for the first time – I had been waiting for this – he swore a sudden volley of earthy expletives.

'From now on, it's white girls or nothing.'

'You've tried that already,' I reminded him.

He gripped the arms of his chair and then let his lungs collapse slowly.

'Why don't you try men?' I asked, refilling my glass.

He stared.

And spat: 'You're full of filth, do you know that?'

'I have long suspected it,' I said, losing interest. But I threw in my last coin: 'Or simply masturbate. We all do.'

Furiously, he – refilled his glass.

We drank in silence for a long, contemplative hour.

'They're going to send me down,' I said.

'What?'

It was good of him to actually sound surprised.

'If I refuse to go into Warneford as a voluntary patient,' I added.

'What's Warneford?'

'A psychiatric care unit,' I said. 'I have until lunch this afternoon to decide. Between either voluntary confinement or being sent down.'

I tossed him the Warden's note to that effect. He unfolded it.

He whistled.

The sound of his whistle almost made me forgive him everything, including himself. Finally he asked: 'What have you decided to do?'

'Be sent down.'

'But ...'

I interrupted: 'It's the one decision in my life which I know will turn out right.'

'Will you stay on in England?'

'Yes.'

'Why not go to Africa and join our guerrillas? You've always been rather more radical than myself and this will be a chance blah blah blah blah blah.'

I yawned.

'Your glass is empty,' I said. 'But take a good look anyway, a good look at me and all you know about me and then tell me whether you see a dedicated guerrilla.'

He looked.

I refilled his glass and opened another bottle as he scrutinised me.

He lit up; almost maliciously.

'You're a tramp,' he said firmly. 'You're just like that nigger-tramp who accosted me the other day when we ...'

'I know,' I said belching.

He stared.

'What will you do?'

'Writing.'

'How will you live?'

'Tomorrow will take care of itself, I hope,' I said.

And that was the last time we made speech to each other over bottles of claret throughout the small hours until clean sunlight slivered lucidly through the long open windows and I left him sleeping peacefully in his chair and hurried to my last breakfast in college.

THOUGHT-TRACKS IN THE SNOW

The skies had been overcast. My affairs were going badly and I was as gloomy as the great grey clouds that hid the sun from view. I had been ill, a fever, and had had to put up with medicines and a great deal of curious attention from my landlady who had taken the position that my writing was certainly not doing me any good. It snowed heavily that Sunday night and I watched the thick white doves' feathers of it come sailing down and pile up everywhere. I could not sleep. A restless refrain was repeatedly flashing through my mind: 'You're crazy, you're crazy, you're crazy.' And great armfuls of it were snowing down on to the roofs, on to the roads, on to the pavements, snowing down into everything: 'You're crazy, you're crazy, you're crazy.'

The week before, I had finished typing out my novel and had sent it off and had thought that I would be free of it. But the thing was oppressing me and I was making the postman nervous and making myself ill all over. I had then pulled myself up sharply and started again, giving lessons to a pimply youth who was certainly not interested in the course he had signed up with me. He came from Nigeria, he said, and what did I think about the Rhodesian crisis and about white girls? And any time I so much as hinted that we were supposed to be paying attention to his unwritten essay on William Blake he would shake his head in such a way that I felt quite uncomfortable. My sessions with him always turned out to be alcoholic bouts because he brought with him not the essays he ought to have done but bottles of spirit which invariably made us quite jolly and talkative about anything under the sun – as long as it was not anything to do with English Literature. He had, he said, read my stories and found them quite indigestible. Why did I not write in my own language? he asked. Was I perhaps one of those Africans who despised their own roots? Shouldn't I be writing within our great tradition of oral literature rather than turning out pseudo-Kafka–Dostoyevsky stories? What did I do with myself when I was not working – did I have a girl? Did I know that I was a shit? No, he said, I did not quite mean that – I meant shit in its good earthy sense.

And outside, the wet snow piled up softly like things which a man has chosen to forget, things sailing down the sky and quietly gathering up inch by inch to bury me. I felt so hot I was unbearably cold. I felt so cold I could not stand the heat of it.

It seemed the teargas fumes were still choking me; the police-dogs still biting chunks out of terrified students; the stones still crunching into fat white faces; and from every side the howling of sirens, the grinding run of boots, the upraised truncheon – in the instant before the jarring of bone beneath polished hardwood – arrested by the camera shutter opening and shutting. Thick smoke erupting over the rugby and cricket fields suddenly covered everything; when it cleared armed policemen and soldiers had herded the students on to the old cricket pitch and a long line of wire-meshed vans was taking groups of students to the emergency detention centres. A group of white students was cheering the police and jeering the prisoners; a Rhodesia Television cameraman was carefully recording everything. The huge Alsatians were licking their massive jaws at the long line of prisoners ...

Thought-tracks in the snow – shit!

As the plane burred into the night, leaving the Angolan coast and heading out into the void above the Atlantic, I suddenly remembered that I had, in the rude hurry of it all, left my spectacles behind. I was coming to England literally blind. The blurred shape of the other passengers was grimly glued to the screen where Clint Eastwood was once again shooting the shit out of his troubles. I was on my own, sipping a whisky, and my head was roaring with a strange emptiness. What was it really that I had left behind me? My youth was a headache burring with the engines of a great hunger that was eating up the huge chunks of empty air. I think I knew then that before me were years of desperate loneliness, and the whisky would be followed by other whiskies, other self-destructive poisons; I had nothing but books inside my head, and they were burning me, burring with the engines of hope and illusion into the endless expanse of air. Who was I leaving behind? My own prematurely grey head still sat stubbornly upon my shoulders; my family did not know where I was or whether I was alive or dead. I do not think they would have cared one way or the other had they known that at that moment I was thousands of feet above the earth, hanging as it were in the emptiness which my dabbling with politics had created for me. I felt sick with everything, sick with the self-pity, sick with the Rhodesian crisis, sick! – and the whisky was followed by other whiskies and my old young man's face stared back at me from the little window. Would Oxford University be any different – was I so sure of myself then? Dawn broke as we flew over the Bay of Biscay; and the fresh white dove's down of breast-clouds looked from above like another revelation that would turn out, when eaten, to be stone rather than bread.

'I meant shit in its good earthy sense,' the Nigerian repeated.

On the little table between us was the forgotten text of William Blake's *Songs of Innocence* and *Songs of Experience*.

A sudden knocking saved me from making any reply. I looked at my watch and knew immediately who it was who had come. When she came in and curled herself up on the rug by the fire and muttered something shocking about the weather, I could see the silent accusation in the Nigerian's eye, an accusation that suddenly turned into a challenge. I could see it was going to be one of those days again. My head was burring again with impotent anger, a sickening desperation which for once I dared to crush.

'It's time for my next lesson, so you must excuse me,' I said breathlessly.

141

All my life I had never been able to control my breathing.

The Nigerian looked up sharply. He decided to let things go; and got up and left without another word. Rachel was staring into the fire; the way her shoulders were shaking I knew she had resolved to do something drastic.

'You finished it?'

Her voice was coiled round the steel wire of a taut self-control.

'Yes, I've sent it off to the publishers.'

She had not turned round. My glass was unsteady in my hand.

'Aren't you going to say hello to me?'

I had not expected this.

I got up and put my hands on her shoulders but she twisted round suddenly and slapped me hard on my cheek. Good heavens – what was it that had happened to her face? I stood there, with my old man's grey head, and knew that I would always be slightly ridiculous.

She had turned back to the fire. Her shoulders – those small frail shoulders! – still shook. I sat down and refilled my glass and remembered quite bitterly the Nigerian's taunts. It was a poisonous comedy the two of them expected me to play.

'Don't you care I've been seeing him? Sleeping with him?' she asked suddenly.

But I was prepared. Though I knew the wound would hurt badly after she left, I was at that moment prepared for the knife-thrust. Did she then really think so little of me?

'Rachel, it's your body, not mine, and you can do what you like with it,' I said.

'You know what you are – a nigger jackass,' she said.

'You don't have to remind me, Rachel,' I said.

'A hypocrite.'

I felt weak with the heady buzzing inside my head; teargas canisters were exploding around my leaping feet. I hurled a paving stone at an advancing policeman –

My glass had toppled over, spilling my spirit on to the floor.

'I just don't know why I married you,' she said.

We had been married for two years but had slept together only for the first five days.

'Perhaps if we had had a child ...' I hazarded.

She swung round, but the fire was still burning in her eyes This is it, I thought.

'I am with child,' she said softly.

She always lowered her voice when she delivered what she thought was a deadly sword-thrust.

'And it's his child,' she added.

I refilled my glass; emptied it; refilled it again.

'That Nigerian boy?'

'He isn't a boy,' she said. 'He's a man, a real man. Not an impotent bastard like you.'

'I'd rather you left my mother out of this,' I said, 'but if you must drag her in, by all means do.'

'I want a divorce.'

'By all means get one, Rachel. I told you seventeen months ago that ...'

'You really think you're superior to everybody, don't you?'

'Now, Rachel, you know that's not true.'

'Don't Rachel me!' Her screamed words struck the ceiling and bounced back on to the bookshelves.

I cleared my throat.

'You never really loved me,' she said.

The note of self-pity in her voice – I recognised it in that far-off Rachel with whom I had tramped around North Wales and been immeasurably happy for five short days. I nodded

143

towards the decanter. And she silently, thoughtfully made a drink for herself.

'Damn it, Charles, why – why?'

She was chewing her lower lip. And then, abruptly, she sat down on the arm of my chair.

'Why?' she repeated.

I said nothing. She was deliberately impulsive – playfully almost – when she chose to be.

'How long have you known?' she asked.

'Long enough not to hurt any more,' I said. The door was opening slowly.

I leaned forward to refill my glass and she circled my shoulders with her arm and with the other turned my face towards hers and kissed me.

The door swung wide open and the Nigerian stormed into the room, cursing: 'You bitch! You bloody bitch!'

'Charles!'

'Fucking white bitch!'

'Charles, don't just sit there – he's hurting me – your wife!'

I tried to duck but the truncheon struck the side of my head.

'Charles! I'm your wife!'

She was down there on the floor being mauled by an Alsatian. Another canister exploded on the wall behind me. Thick white choking gas engulfed me. I held down my breath and lunged at the uniformed figure. Somewhere in the background, my landlady was hovering about with a rolling pin.

I grappled with the Nigerian. He was still cursing: 'Fucking Rhodesians – get independence first, then perhaps you'll learn how to fight!'

He was hurting me badly. I could feel the blood rushing out through my nose. Rachel was somewhere on the floor near the shattered glass case. The landlady cautiously crept up behind him and smashed the rolling pin on his great head. He slumped to the floor, out cold. I was trying to wipe the blood from my face and at the same time trying to congratulate the landlady on her timely appearance when a blinding flash of pain hurled me to the floor.

When I regained my senses, the landlady was slapping my face and Rachel was coming in with a dish of steaming water and a towel. The Nigerian was nowhere in sight.

The landlady reached out for the towel, but Rachel said: 'You've done quite enough as it is. You could have killed my husband, you know.'

The landlady sighed like one who is used to being ill-used: 'It's my glasses. I couldn't see which one was the Nigerian and which one was him, you know. And I thought I may as well knock them both down, because I didn't know who it was I knocked down first. You know,' said the landlady as she peered down at me.

My lips had stretched out in a tight smile; I was trying not to laugh.

The landlady picked up the dangerous rolling pin and said: 'These are very handy, you know. When my husband came home drunk the other day ...'

'That will be all, Mrs Sutcliffe-Smith,' Rachel said firmly.

The landlady winced; and strode out with great dignity.

Rachel stared down at me and – for the first time since those distant five days looked much older, I mean not much older, than the eighteen-year-old she was.

'It's still not late for an abortion,' she said.

She wrung out the towel and wiped the blood streaming out of my nose.

'Did you hear what I said?'

'I'm having dinner with Michael – you remember him, don't you, from when you were training as a nurse?'

'The one with the stammer?'

I nodded.

I corrected myself: 'We're having dinner with him tonight. He's the best doctor in Oxford. We'll mention it casually to him.'

'Rachel,' I added, 'welcome home.'

Thick white doves' feathers snowed down from the overcast skies. Would my novel be accepted? Would Rachel soon tire of me once again? I was still rather weak; but I knew that deep inside me I had said goodbye to Africa, forever. The illusory dawn of the white white snow gleamed with a desolate brightness. Christchurch struck four o'clock. Once more I paced up and down in my study and tried vainly to drive away the startling refrain that was, like a stuck record player, repeating itself over and over inside my head. When I looked out through the windows, hoping to retrace my life's footsteps, I saw that fresh armfuls of snow had covered up my thought-tracks.

A mindless rage seized him. Boiling his brains. The police constable watched him warily. In the distance, behind the concrete wall, music boomed; hilarious shouts, voices enjoying themselves. He had been kicked out of the concert and had been trying to climb over the wall to gatecrash it through the back door. That is when the police constable made his knees tremble. He could smell the alcohol on his own breath. There was blood on his shirt-front, bloodstains from the fight in the concert. A cut above his left eye, a bruise on his right cheekbone. He could still hear the feral grunts, the impact of the fists on his flesh and bone. One moment he was dancing; the next he was the centre of all the brute punches and kicks erupting from every direction. All those many black fists, those fiery bloodshot eyes homing down on him until finally they hurled him out, sending him sprawling on to his face and elbows. In the dark empty street he had picked himself up like a scruffy dog. And now here was the pig, in the guise of this young constable, asking him his business.

The world was always asking him his business. The business in the concert had been about a girl. He did not even know her. He had just begun dancing with her on the packed floor. He had been dancing on his own all night and then suddenly she was beckoning to him, swaying to his rhythm. He had not even thought about it. If you do without thinking the world will try to think out your business for you; with kicks and punches. And this policeman is trying to think out my climbing over this wall, and my bloodstained shirt-front.

It had been hell, the whole week. Alone in his flat eating semolina and soya beans. Trying to write his weekly poem. Feeling suffocated by the stale gas-fire air in the room. Trying to think out the pattern behind the deeds (or lack of them) in his own life. The flat was one of many in the miserable grey buildings off Clerkenwell Road; seedy graffiti, urine stains, shrieking cats. A gaunt derelict, dating back to the middle nineteenth century, it housed a motley rabble of single persons, junkies, dope-pushers, frightened old age pensioners, unemployed men and women. Most were either 'writers' or 'artists'. All suffered that inner city insecurity which had more to do with a grimy mishandled fate than with financial problems. All week he had stayed in, reading endlessly, jotting down notes, refusing to open the front door if anyone knocked. He had started writing the kind of self-conscious 'ethnic' poetry which has its roots in a bogus vanity, employing the nuances of revolt and black pride. When he pared this down to the bone of his own personal experience, the anaemic imagery of self-analysis soon revolted him. Surely, he thought, a more than human event underlies all poetry, a more than human condition. But, of course, this too reeked of that degree of misanthropy which can paralyse the pen. By Friday night he was ready to give up. That is when he had gone to the African concert in Covent Garden. And now a policeman was roughly demanding an explanation which he himself had tried to wrestle into light all the days in his flat. And the pain in his chest probably meant that a rib or something had been fractured.

'Go home and sleep it off,' the policeman had suggested. He tried to answer, but only a horrible gurgling racked his throat. He spat a glob of blood. And staggered away. Friday night! What was there to go home to? True, there were those books by Patricia Highsmith, P D James and Dashiell Hammett. He had been reading only crime thrillers for months now. And those three authors were skilled enough to heal for hours on end the corrosive effects of loneliness. These days he no longer craved the company of other humans. It was too tiresome, too tedious. To enjoy another's company he had to drink himself into that illusory well-being which makes even the roughest contact a

148

welcome and delirious thing. His watch said 1.30 am. He trudged up Charing Cross and stopped at the Kentucky Fried place. He joined the queue of black and white prostitutes who were slyly remarking his bloodied person. They understood and feared this violence which was an occupational hazard for them. Looking at them as the queue inched forward to the counter, he was aware of their sympathy for him, another victim creeping towards his package meal.

It was raining when he came out, clutching his box of chips and spare ribs. The chill gusts blew hither and thither, billowing out his coat, hitting his face with the liquid globules of yet another indecisive London rain. He liked it.

This fresh and cold blast of sanity, soaking him already with its attendant sense of rootlessness, blew into his lungs and dragged out of him some of the night's bitterness. He drank every last drop of it. Before him was the tall YMCA building; immediately to his right was the illuminated fountain, the blue-green water sparkling upwards like a long drawn out yearning, only to fall back to be recycled upwards once more. Like his own expectations. His own ambition – what had it been so long ago in high school and then at university? What was it? It had started in Africa and now found him here in London. Mooching his way in the small hours towards Clerkenwell Road. The wind and rain roared, splashed, spattered around him; it grew stronger, reaching out its many arms to bowl him over. He leaned into it, walking like one wading against a strong undersea current. Listening to the heartbeat within, which was so like the sound of snapping wire. Guitar wires strummed too quickly, by the cynical chill of the small hours – they sang within and without him and he listened dreamily, eating the spare ribs and the chips in the city's dreary wetness. Behind him, and coming towards him, were other mysterious figures who could have been direct reflections of his own life.

Rain!

FEAR AND LOATHING OUT OF HARARE

What is it about Harare? Is it the nightlife, the hotels, the night-clubs? Or the melancholy solitary walk back to the flat when a tawny, almost rubescent dawn is signalling from within the dark confines of another night? For four years I had not ventured out of the City – the rest of the country existed only in news reports about dissidents, cooperatives and Blair toilets, not to mention Binga, where it was reported that the main meal of each drought stricken day was a tray of fried grass.

(I did once get away for an afternoon of Art at Rafingora; and another of incurious awe when *that* lake spilled, the constipation having been prayed out of existence.) Then I had this feeling that I had nothing to offer to any place outside Harare; all those places out there were crying for development officers, literacy advisers, health assistants, teachers – not for writers. It is difficult for a novelist to justify his exclusive devotion to his typewriter when all round him are the harsh facts of grim poverty and the struggle's aftermath. Harare, with her poetry readings, writers' conferences, easy access to international journals and her arts festivals, seemed the only comfortable island for a writer who learned to till, not with a hoe, but with a fountain pen.

Besides, for the first time in my life I was on easy terms with a city's police force; that queasy city paranoia of days gone by had erased itself from the – now – stimulatingly fresh page of independence. The Rhodies had subtracted themselves from all the interesting nooks of the town. I could walk into any hotel without feeling my skin hardening – no need to wear my skeleton on the outside. The only puzzle was I could not make out the nature of those of my acquaintances who actually enjoyed working in the rural areas and *hated* city life. The – to me – hilariously horrible working conditions they had to endure were more than my own Harare nightmares. But they are a cheerful extroverted lot, eager to learn the life and landscape of Zimbabwe.

I, and most of my acquaintances, have never visited Victoria Falls, Great Zimbabwe, Lake Kariba, Lake Kyle, Chimanimani, Vumba and a host of other places. We would never ever dream of doing so – I hope the Tourist Board is reading this and will take appropriate disciplinary measures. Anyway, what can beat a disco fracas at Jobs, a merry romp on the Playboy dancefloor, a Rabelesian Bacchanalia in the Makabusi Beer Hall, a snoring/ drunken bliss in the cells under the eye of kindly policemen, the night and day (almost altruistic) parade of prostitutes, drunks, beggars, down and outs, thieves, con-men, deceiving and deceived husbands (parading to the jingle of cents and crisp protest of dollar notes)? Ah Harare. Its mysterious method of living out of a suitcase, living in anonymously cheerless but expensive blocks of flats, living no longer on borrowed time as in the past but on borrowed money, hire purchase, the black market and the small advances one may rarely extract from the employer's reluctant clenched fist. Harare, where a scream in the night is the signal for all shutters to come down – it's none of my business who is murdering whom. Harare, with the thousands of worldwise schoolgirls tarted up for the lunchtime disco at Brett's and at Scamps, the raucous scenes at Queens, the National Sports Stadium with its visiting bands and its bogus Cerulean evangelists ... But then listen to Donagh, an amateur photographer who also works for the Electricity Supply Commission, listen to him rhapsodising on the visual delights of the Eastern Highlands. Listen to Helmut who runs a sculpture colony in Chimanimani, listen to him talking of the unique landscape and of the spiritual beliefs of the area. Going further afield, listen to Jo, a teacher at Fletcher High, listen to her and you will taste and touch the tormented beauty of Vumba. And there is Flora and Volker whose experience of Lake Kyle, Vic Falls, Great Zimbabwe and

151

several but lesser known dimples of our country has chiselled into their already world-hewn vocabulary an exciting and ecstatic resonance.

A prophet has no honour in his own country. The country's own charms excite no response in the citizen's armoured heart. Maybe that is the explanation. Only the visitor, the expatriate, recognises the awesome yet soothing personality of our country.

But there is a solution. The endless round of drink, dance, film, sex and sleep is ultimately demoralising. One begins to ask: is this all there is to my life? To fall into a huge vat of beer is at first exciting, stimulating – drinkable – but then the hour of drowning approaches.

Emer, Jo and Donagh enticed me out of the vat. A simple drive to Gweru. In all my days in Zimbabwe, I had only known the towns between Mutare and Harare. I had neither the wish nor the inclination to see any more than was necessary for primary school, boarding school, university. After that it was exile in Britain for nine years. And when I returned in 1982 I firmly plonked myself down in Harare as naturally as a fish that's thrown back into *that* Lake which was spilling no more. And I did not want to budge.

But everything changed when I realised I was drowning in my own Hararean indulgences. Anyway, I returned from Gweru last night. It was not like going to Vic Falls but it was a step in the right direction: I was learning to wean myself from the rather flabby, dowdy Hararean breast. And what I will never forget of this trip is: for the first time in my life I went horse-riding. I'm still waiting for the photographs to be developed.

THINGS THAT GO BUMP IN THE NIGHT

I don't know what they gripe about in the suburbs. Perhaps it's domestic servants, tax, the car, who's who at the office. The City Centre has its own unmentionables, not of the third kind though. Should I roam around town, armed not for attack but for defence? Though it's always a good idea at any time in the City, the Law will still have the last word about carrying 'offensive' weapons. Violence in the Avenues is not quite openly talked about; there's a slurring of words, a shifty look and the not quite sure riddle of whether the chap you're pontificating to isn't actually the one who mugged you the night before. After all, the only way to avoid being maimed or murdered by your attacker is not to look him in the face; as soon as he knows you can identify him afterwards, he will resort to measures unspeakable. A guy in Mbare had his eyes gouged out. With a stick, I think.

Recognition of looming violence can spur the feet to marathon champion pace. There is no need to feel a coward; heroism is the privilege of those who are alive. In any case a clattering but swift spurt down Julius Nyerere Way once saved me from a rather well-planned ambush. To be vigilant, to be sure of time and place – any self-respecting Hararean knows the dangerous areas of the City and wisely avoids them – is the only sure way of not being caught by surprise. And surprise is the grease in the attacker's machinery; deprive him of it and he will flounder.

But for those times when a drink is no longer a drink but a knuckledusted fist hurling itself at your teeth, speed of reflex, reinforced by dim memories of manuals on the martial arts, may or may not suffice to keep you out of Parirenyatwa Hospital. But then a bar is full of empty bottles. Grab one, by the neck, smash its bottom off on a table corner and charge right in. It has

153

a wonderfully sobering effect on whoever is trying to bash you all the way to the dentist. For whatever it is they gripe about in the suburbs, the City Centre is more down to earth, nearer the blood and toil of scars and where the hell is the next pint and the bottle opener ('Use your teeth, twit').

When all else fails, don't take it in silence: scream like hell, scream like Jericho was tumbling down, serenaded by a brace of trombones, scream – and, sure enough, the citizens for whom enough is enough will rush out of their flats if only to thrash the assailant to pulp. It happens sometimes. It happened at my block of flats. They had been burgled about five times in as many days. The whole block was simply fed up to *here* with it all. There had been the policy of turning a blind eye, if it was only the neighbours being burgled. This time burglary was happening to everybody; prevention could come only with the demise of the culprit. And when this particular one tried again on the seventh day – the day Himself rested – a single cry of Thief! Thief! brought all the flatdwellers raining down on the burglar's neck. He was lucky only in that there was something left of him, left for the police to arrest and the magistrate to reprimand, convict and sentence. The news must have gone the rounds of the bleak underworld; there has never been a burglary in the area since that incident.

The most obvious victims of violence are women, whether from their pimps, their husbands, their rivals in the trade or from a random, unmotivated passer-by. I witnessed two incidents in one night last month. The first, just outside the International Hotel, was ugly, I thought. A young man was hugging an even younger girl – too tightly, I thought. I was passing by to get to the Holiday Inn. The young man hissed savagely into the girl's ear and at the same moment unleashed a powerful fist right between the girl's eyes. Before she could scream, he hissed something even more savagely. As I walked past the only sound from the girl – seemingly in a lover's embrace – was a heartbreaking sob and a whimper.

154

In the Snuff Box at the Holiday Inn it was the payday week and the 'women' were out in force. As I downed my fourth pint of chilled Castle Lager (I was standing at the bar and there was no one to talk to), I overheard five stout men apparently planning to beat up a woman who was drinking alone in a corner near the exit. Now I knew they were serious. I also knew they could not beat her up within the walls of the hotel. At closing time I told the girl everything. But she was drunk. She listened and, instead of sobering up, became enraged. The stout five glared at her as they went out – and waited for her to come out. I held her back, but she threw me off, declaring no one was going to intimidate her. Then she took off her shoes and defiantly sailed through the gates. An hour later I phoned the police to come and collect her still breathing remains from the tarmac. Incidentally, some days later, I was drinking in the International and she tapped me on the shoulder. She thanked me in the only way drunks thank each other: she bought me beers the whole evening. And when I was leaving she let me know that any time I felt the itch I could have her free. An honour indeed.

Living in the City Centre, you get used to all the species of hell. Sometimes they take the shape of teenagers. Two of them – I was very drunk – beat me up and robbed me of 65 dollars. I remember feeling nothing about the violence and the loss of the only money I had in the whole world (that evening). The incident was just like everything else, a natural event in an unnatural setting. Violence and the survival of the fittest are just another aspect of nature, like traffic accidents or pickpockets and random muggers. In fact, when I was knocked down by a car in Enterprise Road at Christmas, 1983, the only time my feelings erupted against God and his nurse-angels was when I was presented with the bill for my stay in Parirenyatwa Hospital. I only paid the day before I was summoned to Court.

You don't gripe in the City Centre; you grit your teeth and reach for your –

DREAD IN HARARE

Society is sick. I don't take no sickness from anybody. In Kingston, in London, they wiping our noses in the sickness. No way! Society in Harare is sick. And the disease is money. I ain't goin' take no sickness like that. It divides brother from brother, sister from sister, father from son, mother from daughter. Where you got all this mammon ain't no room for loving kindness. See what I mean?

No.

Look at it this way. Babylon is a state of oppression. Babylon is wherever I am, whoever I am, however I am, whatever I am, whyever I be. It's not just out there; it's right in here in the house of my mind. Remember that *The House of Hunger*?

No.

Oh. Let's look at it from the back. Right? Baboon is what rhymes with moon and looks like a human being. Right?

Wee-ll.

Your body's got to eat. That's food. Your mind's got to eat too. That's what? Education and things, I guess. That's where Babylon begins, don't you see? But let's go back a bit. Into history – history is Babylon, you know. Once upon a time millions of my folks were shackled to slavery. Many died in spirit of this sickness. They are the ones around me today. But a few escaped into the hills and fought tooth and claw against the Babylon bombarding into their minds. Know what The Man says? He says, If you think the world is all wrong, just turn your mind back to front and everything will be all right. Now that's the sickness, don't you see? You know it's *no* but you are taught to convince yourself that it's *yes*. That's the sickness; that's Babylon. And, you know, when you know what I know about the sickness they teach everybody to convince themselves that *you* are the one who is sick. And

157

everybody who died in spirit long ago will hurl rocks of insults at what's left of you. See?

(Firmly) I don't.

I can see you're a hard case. Has your head ever been X-rayed by Babylon?

Look here –

Keep your hair on. Anger is impure. Sick. And yet society teaches us all kinds of things, so when we get into situations we *have* to stand on our dignity. They teach you self-respect, but in their image, so that even *what* you think is your own *personal* anger is actually Babylon's anger. Society transmitting itself through your highly strung nerves. Simple, eh?

I'm not nervous –

I didn't say you were.

But you said –

Okay, okay. But when you're talking, do you know *who* is talking? Do you know what voices are in your voice? When you're talking can you hear the first speaking-man trying to utter the very first grunt that became and reverberated throughout the world as the first syllable? And the immense revolution of that! Or when you talk do you just become the tincan transmitter of a sick society? Remember every *true* voice that vibrates through the Brightness of the Air is a recapitulation of the origins and phenomenal development of speech.

I don't understand.

You could, if I could de-educate you.

That's nonsense.

One was crucified for talking what was thought to be nonsense. Yet today all sorts of countries base their behaviour on His words. But what was it speaking through him when he was saying those words? And was it reaching out through him only to regulate the behaviour of a mere forked animal?

(Sneering) I hear you Rastas think he was Haile Selassie.

Oh, that shit. There's a lunatic fringe to every way of life. And of course it's the lunatic fringe that's always used as evidence that Rastas are bullshit. For me Rastas are Resistance, no more and no less. Resistance to all that debases man. Resistance to all that seeks to diminish the common bond of mankind and his heritage. Resistance to poverty, oppression. Resistance to that within the soul which leads to rapacity, cruelty, indifference ... That's why earlier I said Babylon is not only out there; it is also within us ... Let's go back a bit. In Jamaica the slaves who escaped their slavery and took to the hills are the ancestors of all true Rastas. And in the hills they founded their own liberated areas and defended them with their lives and everything else they had. Today, the Rasta looks at society. He does not shake his head. He does not wring his hands. He acts. He acts through mental and physical revolt against everything in his sick society. He mounts up high in the sky and looks down at the City. Looks down with loving kindness. And his loving kindness, when Babylon looks up, seems like swarms and swarms of black wasps. That's why there is dread in Harare. (Sighs) Dread against what? – loving kindness. (Laughs)

You're idealists.

(Thoughtfully) Idealists? Then you have not understood even a little of what I have said ... Idealists? Okay, have it your way, officer. You can take me back to my cell now.

About time too. *Get up!*

(23 April, 1985)

159

Titles by African Writers

Bâ (trans. Bodé-Thomas), *So Long a Letter*

Beti (trans. Moore), *The Poor Christ of Bomba*

Emecheta, *Kehinde*

Equiano, *Equiano's Travels*

La Guma, *In the Fog of the Seasons' End*

Marechera, *The House of Hunger*

Oyono (trans. Reed), *Houseboy*

p'Bitek, *Song of Lawino & Song of Ocol*

www.waveland.com